samfiftyfour_literary
September 2020
Issue 1

ISBN 9798693096677

September 2020
samfiftyfour_literary
Edited by A.K. Bechtold and Dylan Hogan

• Awo Adu • Bingh • Craig Chisholm • James Leo Critchley • Emily Dixon • David Duenas • Alex Fadeev • Maxine Flasher-Duzgunes • Akhil George • Ivan Gietz • Carl Griffin • Cassidy Guimares • Maria Harkin • Hera • Ethan Hornacek • Hannah May Jessop • Shuvangi Khadka • Sina Khani • Francesca Leonie • Alejandro Marsico • Conrado Martins • M. R. Massey • Madeline Mecca • Nathan Rivera Mindt • Lex Mohamed • Miriam Moore-Keish • Mvula Ngcobo • Danica Popovic • Anya Ptacek • Maia Snow • Cassie Premo Steele • Warren Stoddard II • Mollie Swayne • Amarkant Thakur • Francis Williams • Angelo Zinna • Danielle Zipkin •

CONTAINS:
- a fragment, page 2
- lockdown baby and the death of liza minnelli, page 4
- when i'm gone, page 9
- strikethrough #8, page 10
- the woman with the white rose, page 12
- my cat, a eulogy, page 13
- summer city, page 14
- works without faith is dead, page 18
- argentina, page 20
- pixels in a photograph, page 22
- ordinary, page 23
- a return home, page 24
- apocalypse now, page 28
- homecoming, page 36
- russian texas, page 45
- best western, page 46
- this house is a time capsule, page 47
- going no where, page 49
- heat, page 52
- in march we fell in love, page 54
- the amorous arab, page 55
- eels, page 60
- let me quit. now. (please?), page 61
- how to miss a place you've never visited, page 64
- er coup d'etat, page 66
- the twelfth station, page 68
- coffee shop sonder, page 70
- feng shui, page 71
- ghazal, page 75
- suite of gratitude, page 76
- brooklyn summer curfew, page 80
- a space for mobility, page 81
- realistic ways to break up, page 82
- broken eggs, page 84
- peachtree, page 86
- red pork soup, page 88
- in response to listen , page 93

For most of us, beginnings are intuitive. If a child were to ask us to tell her a bedtime story very few people would begin by saying, "Mr. Smith's alarm clock went off at 6:45 AM, the same as every morning. He got up and put the coffee, before going to brush his teeth." There is no story there to tell; the character has not yet met with the tension that creates the anomaly that begets an interesting plot. The story really begins when Mr. Smith takes a wrong turn on his way to visit a new client, thus witnessing a murder in an alley. Or perhaps Mr. Smith misses his usual bus and on the next one, meets the love of his life. Or maybe a long-lost friend phones Mr. Smith and asks him if he can stay with him. The idea is the same: Stories start at the point of disruption, the place where something happens. It is the jarring of the routine that produces the circumstances necessary to prompt the hero to go on a journey, or to bring the stranger into town.

If any year has a story to tell, 2020 is it. It seems we cannot get our feet under us for long enough to re-establish a routine, before something comes along and jars it once again. Sixty thousand people flood Hong Kong in protest. A mysterious illness sneaks into Wuhan. The whole world travels through their computer screens to the crater in the center of Beirut. Wildfires chase thousands away from their homes and everything they've ever known. George Floyd, an unconventional hero if ever we knew one, takes that final journey into darkness, and then whatever follows.

How do we begin to tell the story? How do we lift up the voices of everyone who has found their life changed this year? How do we speak not just of the massive international upheavals our world has faced, but also of the small ones—the abuela who never made it off the ventilator, the little Black boy who wakes up at 3 AM with nightmares? And what, if anything, can be said of hope, of redemption? What of the victories? What of homes rebuilt? What of people stepping out of their apartments for the first time in months, and relearning what it is to see a sky? What of the people storming the streets, putting their bodies on the line for what they believe?

For us, the way we begin is simply to make a start. We begin by bearing witness. We read the words of thousands of people from every corner of the inhabited world. We listen to stories of love and loss and confusion and anger and hope and darkness and light. We try to make sense of how so much can exist all at once, try to piece together something that can do them all honor. And then we give it back to you.

So this, our first issue, is a beginning. We know a little of that already: In the beginning, God created the heavens and the earth. At some point later, we, each one of us, were told into being. That is where this starts: with you, and with me. Together we will continue until there's nothing left to tell.

Editors

a fragment

Writing while the dust settled on a period of unprecedented global destruction, taking stock in the aftermath of the Second World War, Samuel Beckett said: 'to find a form to accommodate the mess, that is the task of the artist today'. In 2020, the mess seems—impossibly— greater; and our means of comprehending it through art seem ever more challenging and elusive.

Given the scale of the crises confronting us daily—in the horrifyingly vivid immediacy facilitated by modern day technology and global connectivity— crafting a response to the world through art seems a dauntingly formidable prospect. With thousands of deaths being reported alongside a remorselessly indifferent PowerPoint presentation, writing a poem feels like an inadequate means of making sense of such sorrow. Seeing potentially millions of people facing famine and starvation in Yemen, I cannot write a word without feeling overwhelmed by my own inability to approach the extent of human suffering unfolding; not to mention my own unsuitability to comment on it while sat at home, at my desk, watching the developments through a screen. The scale of the tragedies that overwhelm our lives in the modern world is too great to be processed and understood properly: doing justice to the enormity of each, individual experience of unbearable anguish is beyond our capacity for emotional response. Indeed, given the fact that it is difficult to escape being bombarded with graphic videos whilst scrolling through social media; and given the ease with which such content can be rapidly shared and interacted with, our ability to be shocked has been somewhat eroded. This is not a new thought. As Susan Sontag so precisely expounds in 'Regarding the Pain of Others', our 'culture of spectatorship' has engendered a numbing of our outrage, a weakening of our ability to be appalled, sickened, or angered by images that should incite such emotions. Hence, the writer is faced with a crisis: how can you represent and respond to a level of human catastrophe that the conventional forms of mimesis cannot contain? In a society addled by a compulsive addiction to instant gratification, and saturated by visual media, how can poetry remain an effective and worthwhile vehicle for engaging with the world?

There is, naturally, no answer to this question; it has been wrestled with since the very origins of the genre. But one way that I have been tussling with this struggle of representation, this difficulty in ordering a mass of events, sequences that defy any attempt to find cohesion: is by making the struggle the very subject of the work itself. Tony Kushner's words have stayed with me, echoing repeatedly in my ears as I have grappled with this COVID-induced writer's block. Writing about the challenges of displaying the moments of supernatural, otherworldly magic on the stage in Angels in America, Kushner states that 'it's OK if the wires show, and maybe it's good that they do." This idea of embracing the theatricality of theatre—not being afraid of its artificiality—appealed to me as a way of approaching writing poetry against the backdrop of global crisis. Acknowledging the imperfections inevitable in any work that seeks to tackle such universal and wide-reaching issues—and making that imperfection the heart of the work—can then become a means of obliquely expressing the size and range of the subject matter being tackled.

And conventional poetic forms are exposed as flawed vehicles for responding to a world that defies classification; is riven by polarisation; and resists any attempt to settle into a calm, unified whole. The poetry of the present moment should be equally dynamic, fluid and unconstrained; it should call attention to its own fabricated nature, and be self-reflexively conscious of its own performance as an attempt (and nothing more than an attempt) at trying to, if not find a 'form to accommodate the mess', at least come closer to comprehending the true nature of what the 'mess' really is. And so the wires show.

James Leo Critchley
Newcastle Upon Tyne, UK

lockdown baby and the death of liza minnelli

Eileen's parents named her after the song. There are lots of things she wishes now she'd asked them before they died, but mainly she wonders if they knew what a dirty song it was. Who would do such a thing? Name you after a dirty song and then die? Inconsiderate. Siobhan said they probably named her because they did dirty things while they listened to the song and made her while they were doing it. Brendan says it's about drugs, but Brendan says everything is about drugs.

Eileen, Siobhan and Brendan used to smoke together outside the stage door. Before that they smoked outside the box office until a member of the public complained. Now they will have to smoke on their flat balconies and out the windows of their childhood bedrooms. The theatre says it will reopen and Brendan says fuck off will it reopen. It's not a cultural landmark, this one. The last act before they closed was a psychic who got the town's name wrong and smelled of gin. The whole theatre always smells of gin on a spiritual level if not a physical one. It has upholstery from the last opium war. It did pay a living wage though.

As she packs up her locker, before they go to the pub one last time, the manager comes over and asks Eileen if she'll be okay. He learned how to do his concerned voice on a course about compassionate management. She's the only one he checks up on, she's the only orphan girl, the only urchin, the only one who didn't go to uni. She is a charity case who fits the establishment's penny dreadful aesthetic.

"Thank you Mr Daniel, but I'll be okay."

"You know you can email me if you're experiencing any distress or hardship?"

"I do know I can email you if I'm experiencing any distress or hardship. Thank you Mr Daniel."

"Are you going to be on your own during this difficult time?"

"I have my Auntie Nora. I'll be fine." Fuck off will she go see Auntie Nora though. Auntie Nora has only eaten Weight Watchers ready meals for fifteen years. She wants Eileen to join a pyramid scheme.

"This is a terrible time to be young Eileen."

"Thank you so much for your concern, Mr Daniel. You're a very compassionate manager."

A lot of shit has accumulated in Eileen's locker. By the time it's packed in two fat rucksacks the pub is almost empty. Everyone must have realised they weren't meant to be in the pub. It didn't seem worth going in. The bags were heavy and the public transport was only going to get more worrying so she went home. She saw a lady on the pavement coughing, but she saw it through the window of the bus from eight or nine metres away so it was probably, probably alright.

Her housemates have already gone, Nina and Alice and the other one. Nina moved in with her asthmatic girlfriend, half out of love, a quarter to do her shopping and a quarter because she has a one bedroom with a bathtub. Alice is trapped in Prague. She says it's terrible and she's very worried. She's staying with her grandparents and they own two Picassos though so it's probably fine. Eileen isn't sure about the other one, but they've definitely cleared out so she guesses they have parents who live somewhere, or something. Eileen is the sole inhabitant of a four bedroom house. She has achieved a million people's property goals. She can exercise naked, she can leave ham unwrapped in the fridge, she can die and not be found for six weeks.

The others have taken half their stuff with them, but half heartedly. They did a supermarket sweep of the living room to prepare for the coming siege. Eileen walks around barefoot noting what is gone and what is part of her armoury now. The throw from the sofa, the toasted sandwich machine, the good fan heater, and approximately fifteen coathangers are all gone. No one has cleared out any food so she will eat all of it, every last bite. She can be a gourmand now. She will eat all the leftover pizza once she has picked off the mushrooms. If she had parents would they have bought her a toasted sandwich machine like Nina's did? Was Auntie Nora meant to buy her one and she's been shirking responsibility all this time? Bitch.

Before unpacking she opens her laptop and types Liza into YouTube. The search bar autofill knows what she needs before she types it. When she starts singing it's the perfect compromise between wanting someone's voice to colour the silence and not wanting to talk to anyone she knows. Maybe Cabaret this time. If Eileen's voice could fill a room like that she'd never be lonely, if she could win best actress in a purple evening gown and turquoise eyeshadow. If she could make looking at her that magnificent, she'd never be quiet again.

In her backpacks from work she takes out four half-finished packs of paracetamol (essential in these troubled times), two stilettos with broken heels, a book she never finished and her favourite feather boa. When Siobhan asked why she had it she said it was for the staff party. She didn't say it was the only childhood dream she'd ever achieved. That's enough unpacking for today. She puts the feather boa on and lies down on her stomach in the middle of the kitchen. Her breasts and stomach smush into the lino gratifyingly. How excellent to have no work, no one to share your house, and be totally free to smush yourself into the kitchen lino in your favourite feather boa. The floor smells of fear and fairy liquid. She is a dying whale. She hauls herself onto her back and feathers gather sparkly in her nostrils. They smell of pink.

"Don't tell me not to fly, I've simply got to." She begins low like a secret. Her voice rumbles across the lino like a wave gathering itself to submerge a city.

How many weeks has it been? Hard to say, but there's mould on the apples now. She'd throw them away but she wants to see what colour they'll go next. Every time she's about to put them in the compost she remembers she lives alone.

Siobhan is crying because now she will never meet the perfect man she found on Hinge just a few days ago. He liked Grey's Anatomy and good wine and she's sure this one can't be married. What if he was the love of her life?

"He probably was the love of your life." Eileen says. She is upside down at the end of her bed in a yoga pose she invented herself. "You'll probably never find love again. It was only him in the entire world."

"Fuck off Eileen."

Eileen doesn't want to go on a date. If she wants anything she wants someone to tell her she's pretty then walk briskly away. She misses being stared at and she misses the customer who asked her to join him in the disabled toilet cubicle. She didn't meet him, but she still likes to imagine him waiting.

"Just think how you'd have felt when you found he was married."

"You're right." Siobhan is nearly twenty three and her greatest fear is running out of time to have a baby. She's never had sex with a man who wasn't married. Why this always happens is a mystery to science.

Brendan says "Mm." He doesn't like talking about men in case he could sound gay, but otherwise he's in a good mood. He recently discovered Hunter S Thompson which was a very meaningful experience for him. They think he feels isolated and lonely but he won't tell them about it, he just goes very quiet. Eileen brainstorms the things she thinks he might miss and wonders whether she should bring them up or not. He'll be missing his gym, he'll be missing second hand record stores that smell of smoke, he'll be missing strange one man shows in theatres above pubs. She went with him to some of those but they made her feel stupid so she stopped.

"Are you alright Eileen?" Says Siobhan. Eileen thinks how they'd love for her to be lonely right now. They'd love for her to be sad like them so they won't feel like fuck ups. If she's doing okay and she has so much less than them, if she's doing okay even though her parents are dead and she's about to run out of money, what does that make them? She knows they're scared of being avocado toast archetypes. She knows what they need from her. They can be a mess if she is a disaster. She wonders if she'll give them what they want.

"I'm very well thank you. Nothing to complain about at all." Maybe next time she'll say she's suffering. They can make her feel better and write in their secret diaries that they helped. "I'm learning Spanish and I've been making soup. It's been a meaningful time for me really, I'm learning a lot about myself and I've got quite into meditation." The looks on their faces.

Shortly after that the call ends and she laughs to herself, upside down half off the end of the bed in the empty room. Maybe the houses next door are empty too. Maybe the whole street is. Maybe she could reach her arms out a kilometer wide and that whole space would be uninhabited, and she can role play Planet of the Apes running down the street in her pants towards the corner shop. Auntie Nora never showed her what to do with time like this. She never learned to bake. She doesn't like soup. For breakfast she ate four gherkins lined up a perfect distance apart on a plate decorated with tiny fancy leaves.

Lonely and hungry feel similar to her. They both start in the torso and radiate outwards. She's lonely in a not wanting to talk to people way and she's hungry in a not wanting to eat way. The house feels different now, it is part of a stranger and quieter nation away from the one the newspapers write about. Other people can go to the shops now or sit two metres apart in parks but Eileen has been given different rules to follow in the dreamworld country. She's a different sort of creature now. Her purpose in life is inhabiting this house alone.

There must be a way to talk to someone without losing the game of not talking. On a Thursday she has an idea. She goes to a website for people no one else wants to fuck and introduces herself as Sally. She tells a man she was addicted to speed in the eighties but she's clean now. She sucked off a Rolling Stone but she won't tell you which one. She has pierced nipples but you can't see. If you look at the picture she posts you see her topless from behind holding her favourite feather boa up above her head. It could be an old photo, she could be any age, it might be a real polaroid or she might have made it with a pretentious app. Siobhan took that picture at a work party when she thought it would be funny if they took all their clothes off. A man had just left her and she was drinking vodka. It turned out he was married.

A man from the website calls her and she answers curled up in a ball under the coffee table. Life's candy and the sun's a ball of butter. Yes, she is naked right now, apart from her stiletto heels, a top hat and her favourite feather boa. She's having fun when she's talking but not when he's talking. She doesn't want to hear what he's up to or what he looks like, she just wants to listen to the silence when he believes her. She tells him he's a pervert and hangs up.

Next time her name is Fanny and she blocks anyone who thinks it's funny. Now there's less food left. She ate a whole box of praline chocolates at three in the morning then didn't eat for twenty six hours to see what would happen. Nothing happened. She nearly ordered Chinese food then she bought a book about sculpture instead. She doesn't go outside because then she would lose. She tells the next man that she had a husband called Peter but he turned out to be gay. It's okay because she meets so many lovely men on the world wide web. This one likes eighties pop music so she blocks him too.

She crawls through the web looking for flies.

She tells a woman from Chicago that her name is Vincente and she has a pacemaker. She thinks the woman is probably lying to her as well.

The bank starts texting about overdraft limits. She decides to drink Malibu and call Auntie Nora in floods of tears. How does she expect her to live without toasted sandwiches? If Nora wasn't such a fuck up, if she sold more vitamins to more housewives, she could finally treat Eileen how she deserves. Then she decides that would be boring and she doesn't have any Malibu left anyway. Siobhan has started karate to help her with her self confidence and Brendan has grown a beard.

In her pyjama bottoms decorated with Christmas sheep and her feather boa, she strokes up and down her ribs between her breasts.

Eileen wonders if she could go out now. It might have been months since she saw the news. She prefers current events to be a surprise. She thinks when it's time she'll build a new world with the other survivors, she'll be their funny girl goddess of valium and Follies. Everything will be different. When the moon is high enough and she feels the curtains about to open, she will be a freckle on the nose of life's complexion. She will step magnificently down the front stairs and sing.

> Emily Dixon
> London, UK

when i'm gone

when I'm gone I wonder
        if they will erect a plaque in my bedroom
that reads
        "A poet slept here"
make the loft a library
which not only allows
but encourages the homeless to masturbate in the bathroom
        with a frankly ridiculous collection
        of French surrealism in the corner
frame the crack in the ceiling
as an abstract art piece
    and offer a peek inside my bedside table
    for £4 per minute
they can have one window always open
for the fatalistic jumper
        and a gift shop by the exit
        selling plastic incarnations
        of John Cena and Jesus

                Francis Williams
                Bradford, England

strikethrough #8

from an inquiry on erasure in choreographic score

I.
reflective italicized
winging feet
and fabric torn and rolling
like ants full of dust
and tumbling
like weeds

what if the embossed
glow of her nylon shorts
swished a midnight blue
fire—her leg a needle
in the hole
fine tipped, spindly

II.
~~reflective~~ italicized————————omit symmetrical hands
~~winging~~ feet————————————insert sickled feet
~~and fabric torn and rolling~~————insert finger sewing
~~like ants~~ full of dust——————enlarge walking increments
and tumbling
~~like weeds~~——————————————insert flower blossom

~~what if the embossed~~
~~glow of~~ her ~~nylon~~ shorts——————insert lacklusterness
~~swished a midnight~~ blue——————insert dawn
~~fire—her leg a needle~~——————insert ash, insert bent knee
in the hole
~~fine tipped, spindly~~——————————insert round body

III.
italicized feet
full of dust
and tumbling
her shorts
blue
in the hole

IV.
italicized feet
~~full of dust~~ ————————————insert leaf blow
~~and~~ tumbling
~~her shorts~~ ————————————insert dance with pants
~~blue~~ ————————————omit ocean, insert canyon
in the hole

V.
italicized feet
tumbling
in the hole

Maxine Flasher-Düzgüneş
New York, NY, USA

the woman with the white rose

    Good evening, I'm the narrator and my name really is Narrator, if you believe that: my mother was one of the first crack consumers of the country. I'm glad I'd let that out of the way already. I'd say that left a mark on me ¿didn't it? I was so destined to become a narrator as someone called Lance Hardwood to be a pornstar. Don't you look at me that way. Doesn't matter, that didn't stop me and, as soon I started, I never looked back. They pay handsomely. So much that people often lose their manners and stop presenting themselves, they say it's more "professional" that way. Well, let me tell you, I know what I have to do ¿ok? And, as long that I don't get myself too worked up by these presentations, everything will be fine, manners will be respected ¿are we clear? Anyway, I imagine that you want to know something about me ¿am I right? Well, I narrated Les Misérables in its time. A masterpiece and one of the greatest novels of the nineteenth century. I imagine too that you have some doubts about that ¿right? Oui I know french, merci for asking; and it could be said that I know a lot of things, everything in fact, about the stories they propose to me. Fun fact: those of us who are blessed with the chance to feed our children with this profession receive what we could call "scripts" to our homes, which give us the good fortune to choose the next project to embark ourselves. That's what was happening with the good ones, at least. The bad ones got little stints in Rashomon-style shit. Nobody wants that. You want to be believed, you want to be believable and, for that, you have to be honest. That reminds me: Henry James, you bastard. I need to say it at least once a day. Frankly, my dear, there's not much work as it used to be. Let me tell you, you could finish telling a story of a chick with a fucking flower like that without even realizing it.

    And that is because a fad is being created again for the last hundred, hundred and fifty years of people talking (I can't, I refuse to give them my title) like they know shit, people that ask to be called stupid names like Ishmael or that they remember a fucking cupcake ¿who wants that? People that are dead, incarcerated, crazy, oh my freakin God, so much batshit cuckoos that is vomiting, repulsive and, to be candid, in poor taste. Worst of all, they took the jobs of the ones that had studied for them, that were instructed in the arts. I went to Cornell, dammit. I am not some hack: nineteen chapters about Waterloo don't narrate themselves for god's sake. I was a God ¿ok? I could've given you lessons about the construction of the Paris sewers until your eyes popped ¿and now what? ¿are we gonna make some fucking collages, call that a chapter? Better yet, let's copy-paste some Wikipedia links: boom, you have a book. Good luck publishing your PDF's, numbnuts.

    The woman had a white rose and then she died. Go fuck yourselves.

Alejandro Marsico
Buenos Aires, Argentina

my cat, A eulogy

I killed my cat. I am 36 years old and cannot keep a cat alive. I didn't do anything sinister, you wont see me on Don't Fuck With Cats 2 or anything. Turns out carelessness killed the Cat, not, curiosity. Well actually if he hadn't of been so fucking nosy he might still be alive, poor Lyle. He was in a whiskers advert in 2015. I named him after the estate agent who rented me my flat. Estate agent Lyle doesn't know that cat Lyle existed, and if he did - both myself and Cat Lyle would be thrown out on the streets. I'm 36, and my ovaries are beginning to cobweb. But don't panic, I have done the strategic, sensible thing and booked a hot date to freeze my eggs. Get those bad boys out and in an ice bucket. A doctors silver scalpel, my eggs, and me. Proper fairy-tale. I may be single, but I will not have this taken away from me. I want to bare a child, and why should lack of sperm get in the way of that? One day. When I'm a grown up adult who doesn't eat custard creams for breakfast. Family parties are a minefield. 'How is the big smoke?' Are you seeing anyone?' 'You're a real career gal aren't you?' It sounds like a question – but it isn't, it's a statement made by a judgemental yummy mummy with baby sick down her back and a lactating tit. Yes Karen, the baby fat IS still there. The fact is, I do care about my career – a lot, but I just haven't met anyone I like enough to make a whole new person with. I often wonder how maternal I am, on a scale of one to ten – if Karen Mathews was one and Michelle Obama was ten, I reckon I would be a 4. I forget to water my plants, I burn food, I leave the tea bag in for too long and sometimes I straighten my hair when it's wet. This is not a woman who is ready for a child, surely. I left the balcony window open, and that is how I know that Lyle is dead. Cat Lyle. Estate agent Lyle keeps sending me emails with flats in my budget so I know he's alright. I live a stone throw away from the M25, it's so close that I could spit and it would land on a car windscreen. He escaped. It's a modest flat, nothing special but its hardly Shawshank. My point is - living with me must be bloody unbearable – because Lyle has risked one of his nine lives to get away from me and start a new life of his own. Good luck to him – shady bastard.

Hannah May Jessop
United Kingdom

summer city

Introduction

I was never born. I was never "myself". People say they change, but people are born from change. I don't know what I am but a medium for emotion. What I feel, all the sound waves and quickly flashing memories of glittery light particles reflecting off of warm brown eyes—they barely qualify as emotion anymore. I am just bits and pieces of things that no one can put together. I am the bright orange of the empty pill bottles that fill up a box under my bed. I am the sound of the Sun screaming in July. I am the jealousy I feel when I sometimes hear a jazz standard echoing down the empty music hall. I am the shaking in my fingers when I feel my vocal cords vibrate with a piece of my soul. I am the gentle violet of my favorite flowers. I am the cold autumn wind which whispers around the city, year after year, round and round...

The House

Mr. President, they tell me you live in a house of white, but you live in a house of green. I've seen your forked tongue and yellow eyes and fangs in every television, every screen, every photograph, every store window that has a sign saying 50% OFF, every billboard, here, there, everywhere. I didn't see you in the desert valley where aliens walked through the brush and over the moon to the next planet over. I didn't see you in the mountain stream where I enviously watched water striders keep afloat as nature willed them to. I have memorized the way your slitted pupils flicker in the camera flash. Isn't it strange? I think I know you a whole lot better than you know me, but you're the one who pulls the strings on this land I live on. At least, you think you do.

Mount Olympus

They tell me that you live on Mount Olympus. We all live on Mount Olympus, where Hermes brings the proles their government assistance checks, and you can see Hercules at the courthouse where you realize his eyes are tired and empty, and you can see Hades cry as spring blooms, and they say if you dream enough you could have a house in the clouds. But I am on no mountain. I live by the river where summers pass with all the grace of a drunken thunderstorm, where Helios forgets to bring the Sun down; he brings it higher, higher, higher, and it gets hotter, hotter, hotter…

The Mine

 I remember the thunderstorm and how I thought nothing of it, because it was just some rain, just the Gulf in its torrential sorrow as it is every summer. I grew up in the eye of a hurricane my entire life. I sang like a canary not knowing I was in a coal mine. For all you talk about coal, Mr. President, have you ever been in the mines? Where your sly tongue and house in the clouds cannot help you any longer? Where the darkness is darker than it's ever been before and even the gloom of your riches cannot compare? Where the cold drills deep down into you, deeper than this chasm in the Earth? Where you are but a lost animal in the darkness of pure black night? Let me tell you: the dust gets in your eyes and you blink but it just gets darker and grittier and you can feel the grime behind your lids and in your lungs but the more you breathe the more you choke and the more you blink the more you're blind and

The Rain

 I saw the rain, Mr. President, four years ago, and I did not fumble for shelter or shudder in fear until I woke up one morning in a pristine white hotel room and heard my dog barking, wondering why she was there. My father told me that there was water in the house, but I replied, no, it was just the summer. Three men died that summer. But that's normal. There were more men. There were always more men. But it was the shaking of the nation which changed the channel. Why, Mr. President, do bullets rain upon all our people? People with homes. People with sparkling eyes. People with daughters and brothers. People with books and secrets and junk that they collect under their bed and songs that they've written but are too afraid to share.

Interlude: I Brought You My Bullets...

 I sang songs of: snow falling on desert skies, I tried, the mirror that can only hold one, reliving our nightmares, doing it again and again, a thousand evil men, I tried, your icy blues, the people in the flame, a stake to the heart, alcohol, I tried, say goodnight, a trunk of ammunition, red is the rose, if they get me, we'll shoot back holy water, skylines, does anyone notice, does anyone care, if I only had the guts, all the things that you never ever told me, give me all your poison, say goodbye. Say goodbye. I still can't say goodbye to him after all this time.

Red Wine

 I saw the rain, but still I thought I was dreaming, until I went to my home. It was my childhood home, where my dog was buried in the backyard by the blackberry bushes, where I once took a sip of bitter, dry red wine, and my father said, "you get used to it"; it was where I cried into my mother's shoulder when she said the house was going to split in two, and where I bled all over the bathroom floor alone until the buzzing went away. What if I don't get used to that taste, where the liquid bites my tongue on the way down and makes my throat itch? I wonder if you ever really cried for us or worried at all, or if you watched how the people all over the country just kept walking down the street to get a coffee or sat in their offices trying to feed the three-headed monster. None of us want to feed a monster, but it's the lesser of two wolves, as they say. We all have to survive somehow.

Ghosts

I remember the smell of the house. It was lonely as it decayed. The carpet squished as I walked in a trance, unable to feel anything. The food in the fridge was rotten and the water everywhere was mixed with sewage and trash. There were people there removing the walls, floors, and cabinets, deconstructing my life into pieces that could fit in the dumpster. Eventually there was only the empty structure full of ghosts and memories, and we don't live there anymore.

North

It's not just me, Mr. President, and it's not just a teenager's melancholy that I feel. I have been to the north of the city where the sidewalks are cracked and uneven, between which wildflowers grow, because they are desperately trying to claw their way out of the cold hard ground. I have seen the abandoned movie theaters, train cars, and demolished gas stations coated in spray paint dreams. I have driven through the neighborhoods with small houses that have screen doors framed by rotting wood. I have heard the pitbulls barking inside and seen their owner shushing them from the porch, which is so narrow that I wonder how they stay holding on. Why, I wonder, are things so difficult to fix, when you live in a house of green with a big neon sign that says "WE THE PEOPLE"?

More Ghosts

I've seen about a million cigarette butts and broken beer bottles ground into the asphalt over the years. Whenever I walk on them, I think of all the spirits beneath them, far beneath them, buried and buried and buried deeper with every new face you have. They call out desperately, crying their phantom song, but no one listens anymore. As time goes on, they get quieter and slowly die away, ever withering, always on the edge, but never quite disappearing. I've seen the hills with thousands of bones within them and marvel at the past. But the past is gone. Do you even remember yesterday, Mr. President? Or did they tell you to Look Ahead At Our Bright Future, Here It Comes!

Chorum Hall

You don't know my world. You live on "Mount Olympus". You don't know the cafe by the university where my father and I had conversations with the sky. There is a mural of a blue town, much like ours, and a white bird. You don't know the smile of my mother. You don't know the quiet room I entered one night in the spring, begging to the darkness in the back of the room that no one would recognize me. I listened to the piano and cried silently. I resented beauty. I resented my love. You don't know about the lake of moonlight where I can firefly-gaze and find flood junk from years past in the forest. Those things all sit defeated and covered in dirt; they are lost, like I once was. The remnants of the past remain, however broken they are. Most things can be repaired. There aren't many stars— they've been wiped out by the great hands of metropolis—but the ones that do look down upon me are bright.

The End

It all crumbles one day, Mr. President. As they say, I wonder if we'll die in flames or ice. I think it's going to be our own fault. Keep your hand on the trigger, because I've seen things, and I'd rather die than live in shackles. They'll forget the ones like me, and you can keep running around in circles until you all fall over and die. They tell me you've changed, but I never liked you much anyway. I play the piano, I live by the river, I live life freely. You could buy the river, but you could never know it. You could buy the river, but you could never love it. Not like I do.

Hera
Baton Rouge, Louisiana, USA

works without faith is dead

dog that's broken beside the door
laughing at death like Christ
on the gay hours of Easter
falling like one, two, three goose heads
on butcher Pete's floor

Mark David Chapman shot John Lennon
in the back four out of five times
sat on the curb
opened up Catcher in the Rye
while waiting for the cops to arrive
(a boring book will drive any man to
kill another)
but God Damn he was a shot
only missing once.

those German boys of the Nuremburg trials
clapping fat hands for freedom
waiting to be hanged or dying
from poison in a cell,
what were we supposed to do with them?

insane women kill their children,
old fruit gets deer drunk in the middle of
nowhere,
zebras only know they're not zebras when you
tell them they aren't,
everyday men and women say goodbye
goodbye
goodbye sweet life of terror
and memories fade like
jobs, cars, women,
anything worth
being saved by.

Mama reads sports illustrated and soaks
bread in vodka as once wise men
now piss all over themselves in group homes

fake Monet's always look better than the
original in a home where a man eats
an undercooked hamburger and screams
at birds on the windowsill

babies say the lord's prayer at six months old
as psychopaths boil leather for dinner
and no amount of consequence will ever
lead you to do the right thing

always shoot your wounded before
you have to,
ducks swim backwards with nothing to eat,
the old movie star makes toast in the bathtub
as the answering machine blinks zero

wrinkles come while
beauty fades
 but not before it has to.

the comedy channel was left
on late

who small am I
to say there
is no
God

says the comedian

everyone laughs.

Ethan Hornacek
West Palm Beach, Florida

argentina

Argentina I am afraid to give you because I know that I will never receive.
Argentina forty pesos and seven cents May 31.
My mind is insane.
Argentina when will we heal the human rift?
Go fuck yourself with your arrogant old age.
Leave me alone, I'm fine with myself.
I won't write anything useful until I feel like master of my brain.
Argentina when will you be worthy?
When will you show a minimum flash of transparency?
When will you declare yourself dead?
When will you own your millions of foreigners?
Argentina, why are your squares full of tares?
Argentina when will you restore your friendship with the neighbors?
I am exhausted of your demands.
When can I go to the kiosk and buy a kilo of dignity?
Your screams ruin my ears.
You make me want to be human.
There must be another way to make this argument.
Pizarnik is dead and that seems unfair to me.
Are you being unfair or am I being excessively demanding?
I try to be concrete.
I refuse to rot.
I didn't turn on the TV for weeks, murders appear every day.
Argentina used to be a liar when I was a kid, I'm not sorry.
I get drunk until the weekdays.
I sit in my bed for hours and insult your inhabitants.
When I'm sober, I daydream.
My mind is made up of illusions.
I am writing to you.
Are you going to let your life be directed by these "journalists"?
I hate them more than you.
I listen to them every day.
They are always talking to me about consciousness. They are aware. Politicians are aware. Everyone is aware except me.
It occurs to me that I am Argentina.
I am talking to myself again.
The enemies attack me.
I don't even have the same chances.
I'd better consider my usual space.
My usual space consists of hundreds of millions of letters printed on yellowed pages of expired books and countless songs on previously discussed topics.

And I don't say anything about the insecurity that not only lives inside me, but is commonplace every time a door is opened and someone goes outside.
I have avoided nightly pharmacies that sell anything but medicine.
My goal is to be like Alejandra even though I am a man.
Argentina, how can I write to you with such honesty despite your hypocrisy?
I will continue as Cortázar my words jump over a hopscotch and seem to be the end of a game.
Argentina I will sell you my stanzas for four hundred pesos and I will give you seventy to buy yours.
Argentina releases Adolfo Bioy Casares.
Argentina saves the poets.
Argentina Bodoc and Piñeiro must not die.
Argentina I am the face of Bulacio.
Argentina when I was a few years old I thought about escaping and donating my ideas to whoever needs them because I feel that in these lands we are demanding because we lack absolutely everything and we have nothing.
Argentina you really don't want to go bankrupt.
Argentina is those evil debts.
The debts want to eat us alive. Its power is evil. They want to get the books out of our libraries.
They want to take our provinces from us. They want the meat in their refrigerators.
That is not right. Damn. They made English our second language. This could be written in your language.
Argentina this is completely serious.
Argentina this is the impression I have for looking at the media.
Argentina, is this correct?
I better go back to sleep.
It is true that I do not want to suffer from winter or hunch because I am sitting in a chair; I do not know how many hours.
Argentina I put my airs poets at your disposal.

Iván Gietz
Buenos Aires, Argentina.

pixels in a photograph

looking hard into the lens of the camera in front of him
an unexpected staring contest which he dared not to lose

he remembered how easily he lost the last one
the camera caught him off guard with a strong flash that nearly blinded him

his eyelids moved to shut themselves in a quick defense
but
it was too late

captured: his eyes had been closed as if he were set for a sweet slumber

Dammit!

he was determined to never be made a fool out of again

my daughter asks me what my father's eyes looked like

i tell her that they were so large
they rivaled the jealous moon
who would hide during the day just to avoid him
they were first responders to his anger
with fire red veins screaming and beaded black pupils constricting in assist
they even stayed open in his sleep
for he was always watching and nothing could get past him

except
for this camera
with a strong flash that nearly blinded him

the last time i looked into my father's big eyes, i finally understood:
the eyes tell the truth in whole
always

if you look someone in the eye long enough, you will begin to see your own reflection
which is to say that you are as much them as they are you

AWO ADU
Cambridge, MA, USA

ordinary

There were about 10 people riding the elevator with me.
Everyone on the way to a class.
A girl, in particular, was carrying a briefcase with one hand
and her phone in the other - besides having a backpack.
While we waited she was editing a picture on it, probably recently taken.
An extremely ordinary picture.

A bird, too far away to look good in a phone camera, perched on some branches.
She slid the saturation of the frame, or some color attribute, from
one side to the other. Back and forth.
The blue gets stronger.
Then the white gets smoother.
Trying to make the bird and the sky in the background pop up from the grey
tone.

She wasn't the only one trying to make a little art,
a little difference, a little bit of new excitement from the routine.
Fuck - I had bought an açaí smoothie that same afternoon. Something i hadn't
done for,
at least,
two months

        Conrado Martins
        Rio de Janeiro, Brazil

a return home
The revolution of Northeastern Syria and its impact on an American volunteer

When you walk into any hospital in America with a gunshot wound, you are bound to attract a lot of attention, bewildered looks, questions. "When did this happen?" Some weeks ago. "How many times were you shot?" Once, sort of. "Did they catch the guy who did it?" This final question proves to be the most difficult to answer, as in reality the man who squeezed the trigger of the dushka that fired the round which hit a wall and then you in many places is likely dead, blown to a million pieces, or captured – awaiting trial or deportation. "I was in Syria," you say, and even more heads in the room are turned towards you. It is like being a novice pianist at a water polo tournament. "What in the world were you doing there?"

Indeed, the first days back in the United States were experienced as one who has never seen electricity before experiences Las Vegas, and this hospital visit was no exception.

I had spent the better part of the previous year in Kurdistan, predominantly North and Eastern Syria as a member of YPG International, far from my homeland of Texas. Surely two sectors of the world must be more different, but if they exist I have not seen them to make the comparison.

I left the State of Texas to journey half way around the world to join the people of Northeastern Syria in the fight against the Islamic State. I transitioned abruptly from towering metropolises to windswept plains sporadically dotted with towns of stout cement structures, from the hectic, break-neck, dog-eat-dog pace of the United States of America to an incredibly leisurely tempo of life in Mesopotamia. I went knowing very little of what I would find in the Middle East. Of course I had versed myself in the ideologies of the Syrian Democratic Forces and its Kurdish wing, the YPG – I knew well the ideals of feminism, direct democratic participation, ecology and grassroots socialism that were espoused by many of the texts I had pored over. But I also had to contend with a propagandized notion of fear instilled into most Americans at a young age about the people and the societies of Southwest Asia. "They'll kill you for your boots," I heard. "Those people just want another American to hold hostage and ransom," I was told. These statements could not have been farther from reality.

Immediately upon my arrival in Syria, I was greeted with a smile and a handshake. "Welcome to Rojava," the young Kurdish man said to me. I could see the white of his teeth bright in the darkness. "Come this way." And I was led into a world which I could hardly have imagined existed there in the arid lands that once were the Fertile Crescent. This society in the crossroads of the world– long plagued by outside influences and domineering nation-states – had adopted its own model of Utopia, and what is more impressive, they put it into action. From the ashes of the war against ISIS, these people had done it. Nearly everything that I had read in the required readings, the manifestos, and the writings of philosophical leaders of the revolution had been implemented in the real world.

The countryside had long been stripped clean by passing empires – Phoenicians, Romans, Persians and Ottomans all played their part in the runaway deforestation that shaved the Middle East. Where once were lush oak groves were now plains in which little grew past a sapling before a passing flock of sheep nibbled the young plants for breakfast. This problem persisted for centuries. Oil derricks outnumbered tree trunks. No trees would grow because they simply could not get the time to do so before being consumed. It was nothing but rolling fields of wheat. The massive undertaking of reforesting Mesopotamia was largely laid by the wayside until recent years when the people of this land set to animating those ideals long collecting dust in forgotten tomes. They began to plant. And it took little time at all for the effects to be noticed – there is a reason, after all, that they call this the Fertile Crescent. The soil between the Tigris and Euphrates is so rich in nutrients, the sun shines so brightly, and the rains fall so heavily in the wet season that the growth of any plant could be likened to a beanstalk. Now, where the rolling sunbaked plains once butted up to the periphery of villages, the passerby can rest in the bower, seeking shelter from the sun in pleasant copses of shade. Creek beds and river valleys exist as massive veins of green, carrying trees and water to the people and cities of the land.

Walking down the streets of those cities in Northeast Syria, an observer unfamiliar with the political framework of the region would be baffled at what they saw – women without headscarves in the Middle East? Churches next to mosques? Vendors selling produce that far outnumbered the amount of suicide bombers?

What we have been learned to accept as a stereotypical reality in the Middle East has been unilaterally shunned by the Syrian Democratic Council. Women lead many of the political wings in the region, making up more than the charter-mandated 40% of the government. Their children, Muslim or Christian go to school side-by-side with those of different faiths, Arab children learn Kurdish as a second language; Kurdish children learn Arabic. And from the bottom of the society on up to the top, citizens are deeply involved in the political decision-making process – a democratic society situated in the heart of what one once considered to be a corner of the world reserved for oil-hoarding dictators.

And what's more, the people of this country – of war-torn Syria – are happy. Happy in the midst of the twenty-first century's bloodiest conflict. Before the Turkish invasion in October 2019, this corner of the country had been spared much of the unrest other regions have had to deal with in the previous decade due in large part to its democratic mission. ISIS, as it was pushed back, territorial Caliphate shrinking ever more until it was nothing but a graveyard, left behind a long-suffering and war-weary populace yearning for peace and stability, yearning for a voice, and yearning for the right to pursue happiness however they saw fit. The result has been harmony edging on brotherhood between these constituents.

In the streets of the larger cities, shops' goods spill out of the stores' walls and onto the sidewalk – set up in a dazzling array of color and scent – oranges here, bananas there, spices, and baked goods. Competing shop owners wave hello and shake hands with one another as they roll up the doors to start the day. If one vendor does not have something, they will point you in the direction of one who may. Though they all sell many of the same goods, there is no single chain of businesses: no Walmart, or Target, or Walgreens, or anything of equal status as a corporation exists in Northeastern Syria due both to the near worldwide trade embargo imposed on the country and its socialist leanings that drive to allow for the flourishing of small businesses.

It is needless to say that row upon row of McDonald's and Starbucks felt as foreign to me as not having a rifle in my hand when I returned to America nearly eight months later, now wounded, now carrying the good and the bad of this place with me. In a sense, I was not happy to be home – the America that I had grown up hearing heroic and noble tales of seemed to have fallen away in favor of an America dominated by corporate greed and asset interest – a country where corporate lobbying controlled the actions of the government instead of the will of the people. The mere fact that thousands of Americans volunteered to fight against fascism in Spain in the 1930's – a civil war eerily similar to Syria's, and perhaps only a couple hundred made their way to the Levant in the 2010's despite vastly improved methods of transportation speaks volumes to this. To me, it felt that America had lost its way, that the US of A was no longer the obvious light in the dark that it had once been.

But what I considered the "American Dream" was alive and well in Rojava.

And in the hospital, flocked upon by bewildered medical personnel, home seemed a very lonely place. Who could understand any of this? There are very few. One nurse lifted his sleeve and showed me a scar. "Taliban sniper did this," he said, "So I get it." But did he? He understood the war, sure, the pain and the bloodshed and the screeching burning seething anger and everything terrible and addictive about the human urge to fight, but what he was fighting for were values won and defended hundreds of years prior – so far removed from present day motivations that they ought to be stored on a museum shelf and spoken of as one speaks of the merits of steel armor versus leather in regards to stopping arrows. The newness and tender vulnerability of revolution was gone from his fight, the desperate urge for success replaced with complacency and greed. Defend the oil.

A story: a Middle-Eastern society seeks to establish a bastion of democracy between the Tigris and the Euphrates, and it is helped along by a world superpower until it becomes inconvenient for the superpower to do so. Money interests, nation-statism take over. Then the revolution is cast to the dogs, left to fend for itself in an arena stuffed with sharks and venomous snakes.

The revolution of Northeastern Syria was not so very different from our own in 1776; a downtrodden people pushing greatly for the right to life, liberty and the pursuit of happiness. Americans would do well to study the society there, perhaps they will find something they might have forgot. Perhaps it is something of value – that place. More than sand and death. Perhaps it is a light in a corner of the world known for its oppressive and omnipotent dark. Perhaps it is a light worth preserving.

Warren Stoddard II
Birmingham, Alabama, USA

apocalypse now

Channel 101, Some Jazeera
    This is some Jazeera, reporting at the dawn of time from the frontlines of The Holy War.
    "AMERICAN TROOPS HAVE PULLED OUT OF SYRIA ALLOWING TURKEY TO MASSACRE THE KURDISH RESISTANCE"
    The bloodhound president of the freedom-loving states of America
    Has moved his men further west so that the angry men
    Of Middle Earth can fight each other to the death

Channel 102, Rox News
    Advertisement Slot
    "Do you need a break from the blood bath of today's news?
    Freedom Mart Inc now delivers right to your doorstep
    Fried chicken to the beautiful AR 15 is just one click away."

    In tonight's debate with Ronan Jelly
    Is there life on Mars?
    Life inside the homeless man?
    Are the savages of Middle Earth really people?
    Can a Saudi bomb split baby brains in Yemen?
    Can the divine stick of Sadam part the sea of oil?
    Can a kaboom from a burka stop an American gun?

    Just in: IRAN HAS YET ANOTHER MAD SUPREME LEADER TO LEAD THEM BACK INTO THE DARK
    Here come the planes!
    American planes?
    Made in America?
    "Come to us," the planes said
    Let me love you
    With my military arms!
    My petrochemical arms
    Don't mind the planes

The smoking planes.
And your burning people
Come to us with your toys and guns
Now that your mother has gone
It's time to pray
But the bomb blew your mosque up yesterday!

Channel 103, BBR News
   Just in: CONSERVATIVES ATTACK GAY RALLY WITH A WEAPON CHILD

The weapon child of the small-minded
Is all over the streets!

Cover up the naked woman
The weapon child is watching
And he might get his eyes dirty!

Cover up the gay man,
Cover up the free women,
Cover up the internet,
Cover up the TV,
Cover up the lovers.

The weapon child is watching
And he might get his eyes dirty!

"Exclusive! Channel 103 will interview a school shooter."
Food for your bloodthirst

"I am the healthiest of the men alive
I am the best of the men alive
For a madness rages inside the TV!
How can any sane man be immune to this madness?
And the raging hell burning in your living room?

How can I get big phallic daddy to listen to me?
It's shutting down, business as usual.
I summon hell.
Into his school and
shut down. Business as usual.

So, I took a gun
And popped some kiddy skulls
And channeled hell into American kids.

Hell was not summoned from elsewhere
Neither did I throw them into it
Hell is carried inside each man of America
Sealed within their insides, hell awaits
Waiting for the day to come.

I am no poster child for America
Neither did I shoot the children of America
America shot its own children.
America shot all the children."

Advertisement Slot
Do you ever get tired of shaving with the same blade?
Again and again and again?
Guilty about discarding plastic razors?
Green America presents
Bamboo toothbrushes and bamboo shavers.
For the green man inside you.

Channel 102, Rox News.
   Just in: THE APOCALYPSE IS COMING! THE SKY IS FALLING FOR
      THE IMMIGRANTS AND THE ANTICHRIST ARE COMING TO AMERICA IN CARAVANS
   There have been several protests by lovers of President Orange.

Channel 103, BBR News
"Today we have a white man with us You're watching the Nazi witch trials
Exclusive to BBR News
All Nazis love Mr. Orange!
Maybe the white man is sexist too?
Perhaps the white man is homophobic?
Burn the Nazi. Burn the white man."

Advertisement slot
Here at Apple, we think of everything
Our users need
So, here's a $1000 emoji machine
To fill the void
The emojis move according to your face
It comes with new studio lighting
To trick your tinder lovers.
The future of catfishing
Upgrade to the new Apple iPhone X
(Terms and conditions apply).

Man screams "Allahu Akbar" and kills everyone at the station
The brown bearded man
Open fired on the masses
Screaming, "Man on a cloud."
And killed everyone
at the station.

Channel 310, N TV.
Unplugged: Music for every mood

Turn up the boom box!
The great gas leak
And the homecoming
Of the great doom
Must be celebrated!

Channel 333, art and culture today
    President Orange opened the twenty-first century art museum of freedom

The freedom lovers have opened an art gallery
There hang the insides
Of babies from Yemen (tomorrow's kaboom makers)

The next exhibit is the corpse of a news reporter
Plated in gold, with love from the kingdom
His throat was cut. He had blasphemed against the lords of Saud
And this gold exhibit earned the Saudis another 100 warplanes

A deafening BOO for the next exhibit
This one is the head of a great terrorist
Who ruled the sand nations and ate white children, boo!
The brave president struck him from the sky

The last exhibit is in fractals
Teeth and eyes from the brown men of Middle Earth
These are abstract; art-lovers can make of it what they want!

Channel 890, international geography
    Today, we have travelled to the most fashionable land in the world

The Souq of Baghdad.

Some attar for the general?
For the perfumes of Arabia
Are known to wash away
the stench of baby blood.

The streets of Kashmir

Pellets shot at young eyes.
For tomorrow's rebellion must be blind

All the pellets must be shot at little eyes
For Mother India

The markets of Gaza

How can you read
the bloody news
if a bomb blew
your school up
yesterday?

Chanel 333, art and culture today
Art and culture are back! Bringing you the latest gossip and news.

An exhibition
Is opening
In the center of town
Trendy caskets
And much more!
(9.99/adult
$5.99/child)

Painting graffiti on the caskets
Creates a postmodern art piece

All the colored caskets
Floating in the oil sea

A scarecrow dressed in a burqa
To ward off evil men.

We have more news from Baghdad
Of another splendid fireworks show

The babies can choke
Their frail lungs can fail
The black air can cloud our waking hours
But fractals must be erected in the skies
For beauty. For awe!

Channel 909, adult entertainment
    Do you get off on angry men ripping off heads?
    Two Bastard Men, One Holy Land ($99)

    Do you get off on dead Jewish children?
    Hamas and Friends ($100)

    Does waterboarding a circumcised man turn you on?
    Adventures in Guantanamo Bay ($88)

    Do you love to see homosexuals being thrown from roofs? A feast for your bigotry!
    ISIS and the Gay Men ($89)

    We've got the perfect collection of DVDs imported directly from Vietnam
    Each one specially tailored to your sexual fantasies

    Are you a man of unusual interests?
    Do you like being watched while you play with your wife?
    Simply use your search engine.
    We at the NSA will gaze
    Straight into your living room
    To feed your voyeurism

    Are you a man of nature?
    Of trees? And Koalas?
    We have the burning Koalas of Australia
    Burned and shot (to put them out of their misery, of course)
    (Only $77)

Channel 01, God TV

Our ministry is working very hard to solve today's mental health crisis! Do your friends call you a bigot for defining your identity by the color of your skin? Do gay people make your stomach turn? Do you want to shoot your liberal friends in the face? Do your nonbelieving friends make you want to slit their throats? Have you been discriminated against for heckling a gay rally? Are climate change activists causing you anxiety?

Call out to God
God and only God
Can save you
Donate to our pastor
So, he may save
The mental health
Of poor tortured souls like you
In his private jet
Donate today
Donate to God

Akhil George
Guildford, UK

homecoming

A mentor, a teacher or some other authority figure once told me that there are two kinds of stories: hero leaves town or a stranger comes into town. Well mine's a lesson in how to be both. A story of a hero coming back to town — as a stranger.

That stranger is me. Everything I say comes with a pinch of salt. Not because I want to lie to you, nor, for that matter, because I particularly don't want to. The truth is that I no longer can tell this one, or any story, without a little bit of fabrication. You see, stories are told in words, words belong to languages, languages belong to peoples. And I am no longer a man of the people. My head is a tropical storm of words, sentences, some sort of images which don't quite fit or belong or make any coherent sense. Out of respect to you, but more importantly, my own crippling sense of ineptitude and delusions of grandeur, I shall restrain myself from building some pretentious conceptual hubba-bubba gifgaf zippity doo dah labyrinth of words in five different languages. Let's stick to the disappointingly narrow limits of this one.

After all, I am a man just like you and probably if we spoke in person some of you would find me obnoxious because of the way I pronounce certain words or my occasionally excessive hand gestures. Some of you would feel inadequate that you are shorter than me, and some of you would think what a nice round ass I have. What you'd know for sure of course, if we met in person, even without conducting a thorough physical examination is that I am undoubtedly, positively and one hundred percent a woman. But female heroes are unstable, tedious, period-obsessed bores. So, I lied, this time on purpose, to grab your attention. Did it work?

I took the bus home. Home? Back into "town" if you prefer. Not because of romance or landscapes or some such crap. It was cheap, and I knew my luggage would be 'overweight' by the standards of any airline. In a world obsessed with bodies (be it negative or our brainwash mantra of the day: p.o.s.i.t.i.v.e), there are few things as embarrassing as being told, point-blank, that something about you is overweight. I admit, it bothered me, and not just because I am a woman. Although, you guessed it, that is probably a lie too, because men don't worry about weight. The worst of it all is that I left a whole bunch of things behind and packed what fit of one life in a big fat slob of a suitcase.

I had a burger in McDonald's at the station. I think that particular station in that particular place is of the particular pre-hipster era of time, still surprisingly small and badly equipped with consumption possibilities. MCD was just a kiosk, with a limited menu and an even more limited staff in the form of one frightened looking black guy who fried chicken nuggets with one hand and counted change with another. I had a plain burger because I thought it was so

Kerouac. After about ten minutes I forgot about Kerouac as I struggled with the familiar digestive sensation of having eaten a block of rubber.

The bus was exactly what you'd expect from a bus going to the place where I was going. Guessed where it is yet? We were late with our departure some twenty minutes because a man, a gypsy, as we like to call them over here without the slightest disgustingly hypocritical sense of political correctness you guys have, paid his ticket and took his seat. The problem was of course that the driver was one hundred percent, positively and undoubtedly sure that the gypsy's sole intention was to use the bus toilet for a smoke and a number two (repeatedly throughout the journey). Both vices (passions?) apparently cancelled his right to buy a ticket and board the coach. Ordinarily, I'm all about self-righteousness but the thought of the aroma (not that of the cigarette), on a sixteen-hour ride immediately murdered the little man-cricket someone once called conscience.

With vibrant approval from the other passengers, the man was escorted out, stumbling as though he'd been drinking and lighting a ciggie as soon as he stepped down from the bus. Well, he was at least guilty of that, said the cricket.

Sadly, it soon turned out he was the least of our problems. Wifi was an abstract concept, air conditioning served with the smell of exhaust, seats broken and the space simply insufficient for three pieces of hand luggage belonging to each passenger. I listened to the mumbled announcement for a few minutes, just long enough to establish that these were the terms we somehow agreed to and that (inevitable) toilet stink was a big bullet we managed to dodge so we ought to be happy, sit back and enjoy the ride. We are going to… and we all know how long it can take to get there. I switched the music on and shifted to the side, turning my back to the people around me. I am a rock… in a safe little bubble that, save for the smells, none may penetrate.

Popular music – in an attempt not to lie to you any more I won't make this claim of classical music – is a perfect package of instant emotion. Melancholy, self-reflection, self-indulgent contemplation of God, universe and the world, down to frenzied exaltation and sexual climax: they've covered it all. I've long had this idea that a great movie scene would feature someone being aggressively unhappy (possibly taking a lethal amount of anti-depressants or trying to slash their wrists with a blunt knife), against Katrina and the Waves' *I'm Walking on Sunshine*. No? Well maybe it's not the most original idea, I never said it was mine.

Music used to be one of the few things (one of the few, if not only thing we're allowed to express opinions about without offending anyone). But then, now, at some point like most aspects of my so-called personality, it became this changing loop of ten songs I discover and rediscover while YouTube gives me just enough of gentle nudge: "Watch it again". There, I've revealed what outdated channel I use to listen to music. That must be at least a little bit original? Well maybe it's not and maybe I'm just clutching at straws here. Bibbidy bobbidy boo.

My nap was interrupted by the woman (one hundred percent even though I made no thorough checks) sitting next to me. She had one of those incredibly kind yet painfully stupid faces, the fortunate type of people that get walked over all the time without ever realizing it. Not that it matters, I think, this whole power-play thing is irrelevant when you don't know who you are or once you finish high school and get over not being popular, you immature manbaby womantoddler.

She looked a little bit like Hans Moleman from *The Simpsons*, with the huge round glasses cutting into her chubby cheeks, always slightly raised because she smiled a lot. She must have thought I was some kind of one hundred percent young lady, the old-worldly type you don't see anymore, and I guess she must have thought, as anyone would have in her situation sitting next to a one hundred percent… that I was less accustomed to the smell than any one of them.

'Are you hungry?'

I took my earphones out and said pardon even though I'd heard her perfectly well the first time round. I didn't want her to think I was a fraud. I told you – if you met me in person you wouldn't think it either. She repeated her concern and when I said I wasn't, she lifted her large reusable carrier bag and started to rummage through. She'd packed everything neatly, in little bags and containers. Maybe not brains but experience told her she at least did not have to contribute to the symphony of scents that was being developed with each passing hour.

Biscuits and sandwiches, and the more elegant mozzarella balls with cherry tomatoes. She was especially proud of the mozzarella for some reason, and although I like it (or did), I didn't take it because I wanted her to have it. I took a tomato (shame to let it shrivel in the heat) and thanked her. Of course, she immediately tried to make it personal and asked. I said it's been a while and I was going home. She sighed and said her daughter was coming *back* from visiting her daughter.

I had no intention of discussing the meaning of home with her of course – the only thing that mattered was that I didn't speak with an accent. Which naturally meant *home* was at the end of this particular road and however long it would take to get there. I don't usually read on the bus, I used to get sick, but now, knowing what I don't know, I realized maybe things were changing in that department and I evolved into a human capable of reading in a moving vehicle and not barfing. In other words – I took out my book. It was in this language, this one right before you, or something similar of course, because I can't remember who wrote it and where their accent came from. As far as I know it wasn't my intention to use it as yet another filter between me and *them*, but it kind of worked out that way and I guess I was just a little bit pleased. If you wish, you don't have to trust me on that one.

'Excuse me, miss?', it was a timid, quiet voice, almost like a child's, yet husky, unmistakably that of a smoker. I realized it came from the man behind me, so I had to turn around, lift my head up a bit to look at him. It was very inconvenient, I can tell you that much, and *that* you better believe.

'I noticed you were reading in (name of the language everyone understands)?'

'Ah yes... short stories by...' (Does it even matter if I lied to you on this one?)

'I used to read in _____ as well. To practice.'

Of course, I didn't believe him. I mean you should have seen him. He was old, older than your grandma for sure, if she is still alive. But unlike your grandma he was aged by the sun and the wind, the skin on his forehead had those sharpei-like wrinkles. He had dark eyes, which to me always seem a little more intelligent than blue eyes, even though I always fall, romantically, for the latter. The point is that he was old, bold and looked like he worked in a field. He wore one of those knitted vests that people wear in this country, in the country. Another hint for you. I smiled, nodded and turned away. You're free to believe him if you like.

***

After dark and a couple of gas station breaks the atmosphere was getting much livelier. One thing you should know about these buses (unless you already do). There's always the one king of the road, the middle-aged man who clearly is still a schoolboy, sitting in the back, wisecracking and entertaining the seventy to one hundred percent women around him.

The lack of certainty in this, larger sample is not again due to detailed physical examination, nor of social identification, although a more backward mind may consider moustache to be a rejection of traditional gender roles. It is merely a matter of biological damage – a woman who, in this particular context does not look, act or nurture like a woman should, can and won't no longer be considered an undoubtedly, positively one-hundred percent. Now you might say the same about me considering I exist...ed on very formal terms, yet these terms in this particular bus in this particular group of people belonging to a people or dare I say n.a.t.i.o.n, despite everything I was as much as a woman as the busty, nourishing, mentally-lactating Mrs Hans Moleman, proud owner of mozzarella.

The man, despite his what people younger than me (relatively speaking of course because I am nothing if not a late bloomer) might call advanced age was, by the very same logic, unmistakably, evidently and boy-could-you-smell-it a man's man. A tribe leader so to speak, he moved his wife to the seat in front so he could have more space and still it didn't seem to be enough. He was the biggest, loudest, and I can only assume that prostate problems did little to diminish his overall sense of manhood. I admit (to you) that I did take my earphones out because I wanted to hear him talk. What can I say, even sitting down he had a kind of stage presence you can't really ignore. And I'm a sucker for good showmanship.

He was obviously telling his life story. How he arrived *there* from "there", how he had little to no money, but he had guts and he wasn't bad looking. And so he and his brother paid a couple of girls (broads, skirts, dames whatever the old man word equivalent in this language is) to get married to them so they can get their papers. Turns out even fraud (much more elaborate yet astonishingly easier to express than the one ongoing) was more romantic then. Because the broads, skirts or dames didn't divorce these two losers, instead they had their children. His was a son.

The business took off (I can't even make up a good enough lie to try to imagine what that entailed so let's call it import-export), and the family was doing well. The normal human condition brought him and the missus closer than either had expected at the beginning. But, as in every good story, fate took its tragic turn. The woman got ill and died, and shortly after (he uttered this in an almost shocking instance of half-whisper) his son was killed in a car accident. Only twenty years old.

I'd probably be lying if I said the bus became perfectly still. After all your perfect still is not mine, mine is more like a gentle humming noise in the distance just loud enough to make you feel that you're never ever alone. Big family, you see. But it was stiller, quieter, there was a kind of dramatic pause, only I can't tell how long it was or if the dramatic intensity was equally distributed across the bus.

'The point is, you mustn't be angry with God,' he mumbled. 'I used to be angry for so long… and it brings no hope or resolution, only despair.'

I wasn't sure whom he had spoken to, but his wife (what I now learned was the new one), gave him a gentle compassionate look, probably not one hundred percent honest, as she must have grown at least five percent tired of this particular story in all its heart-wrenching glory. Me – I realized I haven't heard the word "God", spoken this way, with this intended meaning, or at least this unfiltered, unambiguous hope that someone somewhere is one hundred percent there and listening and understanding… I haven't heard it in over two years and I felt shook.

'So you get a (insert n.a.t.i.o.n. adjective) pension then?'

'That's right. But there is a trick!', his voice grew with a confident crescendo, 'You don't really have to work the whole time, I know a guy who knows a dame who sorted it out for me. Been a pensioner for over six years now, and I'm only sixty-three!'

His voice changed back almost instantly, practically insulting after… You're one step away from this great epiphany and then this person in front of you, this preacher-like figure takes his clothes off. Get it? Like falling from the stars right into a puddle of mud. Maybe that's dramatic and great showmanship but I was angry. Because he was ugly, and a fraud, and so fucking bound in these stupid constraints of some sort of, dare-I-say *people*, yes people, that I knew so fucking well.

I chose to drift away. Into the comfort of instant emotion, the vague directions of personality that no matter how clumsily, pieced together still seemed to make up an existence. My existence. I used to read Dostoevsky every time I felt stupid, and found that he repeatedly taught me something new. But then I got to the point where I'd only read F.M. so I stopped until earlier that year I'd picked up *The Demons* again. It's not a direct quote but it's along the lines of 'A man without a people cannot know God.'

Where I come from, and ironically the human-looking livestock sharing the bus, this was an unacceptable, backward downright evil notion. Because somehow sometime in the not-so-distant past, we started keeping up with the trends and with the rest of the world. And the demons of today were the ones who thought like this, the crazy, the extremists who died and killed for the sake of something which was proven to be an outdated concept in a metropolis where every twentysomething wants to be, and where we all learn what it means to live.

Maybe our God wasn't the same. His took away his son, mine made me annoying and shallow. And yet it wasn't the tragedy per se that pierced through my cold hollow shell of a quarter-life crisis. It was the sense that he, this disgusting man, understood there was something bigger than us, as did I, and to Him we were the same. And only then I looked closer and realized that though everything was going against us, me the troubled, young certain percentage of a woman whose recent experiences changed her world, and this ordinary, no bullshit man's man, man of the house had something in common. This special quality – not the same God, nor even remotely the same understanding of that concept, emotion, belief whatever you pretentious fucks decide to call it. It was actually the slightest thing. The way we both looked up then, through those dirty windows of that smelly bus, out into the darkness, hopeful that someday we can and will find peace.

***

We stopped at a gas station and I went out to breathe and write all of this. That's a lie, I wrote a couple of sentences so I don't forget – I guess the bit about the man's man. The rest is fabrication and editing. While I was writing though, a safe distance from the rest of the heard, the *new* wife approached me. She was one of those good-looking broads, dames or skirts, that always stay good-looking, even old, fat and wrinkly. She probably wasn't more than ten years younger than him, yet she had a distinct trophy wife quality. Blond with blue eyes. She looked down on me, being a younger woman, with a big nose and not a great smile, and I looked down on her in more ways than one, even though her shins were probably in line with my eyes. I was sitting on the floor.

'What are you writing?'

'Oh, just a sort of travel diary,' I said slamming it shut, because I'm terrified people finding out what I write about them.'

'Huh… and I thought you were a reporter.'

That *huh* if you missed it, was the onomatopoeic representation of the bitterest, sincerest disappointment, a confident, happy-go-lucky women like her could express. On my end, it was a mix of pretty-pleased-with-myself 'How dare that stupid bitch think that I, *the marvelous writer*, could be something as common as a reporter', and an unpleasant tingling along the lines of, 'If I were a reporter, I'd probably be writing more, earning more, and would have gained the respect of at least one more person, even if it were this barely-literate, nail-polishing, uncultured cow.'

As she was walking away I saw all of them looking at me, intrigued, puzzled, or at the very least as someone worth making a remark about. I don't think I've been looked at that way in two years. Lovingly perhaps. Lustfully, most definitely. Annoyed – well you can guess that. But with interest? Genuine, where the fuck did you come from and what the … are you doing here? No, not really. This was not yet the town, but I was without doubt a stranger.

***

The driver woke us up (not me) and not-so-gently told us to step outside. It was of course a given, and out here, we were not a whole lot more than cattle. Somehow, it always felt like a very serious thing, and I caught a couple of concerned glimpses – a familial fear over that extra bottle of alcohol nested in their dirty laundry somewhere. We formed an orderly queue, something they never do, and put our best foot forward. Tired, but quite obviously law-abiding. A couple of them had *your* passports (or ones similar to yours) and they held them so the rest of us/them could see. Why would you care which particular ones? It's like attending the same football match – some seats come with complimentary champagne, some offered a closer look at footballers' ugly mugs. The game still had the same score.

I knew a few of them were surprised when I stepped forward, looking over my shoulder, to discover I wasn't on this exclusive guest list. Suddenly I was the disappointing showman. Or maybe that was my paranoia? Either way, on this side, it hardly mattered. My paper was fine. Not remarkable, but fine. It felt like being on a conveyor belt. The Clerk checked if all my parts were in order, they were, and Clerk was glad to see me go.

When we crossed over though, to the *other* side, to *this* side, I immediately felt different. It felt like a different world, and I had a different part to play. There was a woman, and I remember her so well, because she wasn't just a clerk.

She was a hundred and ten percent woman, with eyebrows plucked too thin, dyed black hair tied in a ponytail. She was someone I could know and in a way I knew her. She was a lady police officer, a girl I wished I was, a woman I'd never want to be. Objectified by her colleagues, but made stronger by it, and someone who knew exactly what she wants, and knew how to convey the message. She had long nails, an engagement ring, though that might be a lie.

You see, on *this* side, I was always on the receiving end of two types of looks: 'Who the hell do you think you are, fucking world traveler, spy, you think you better than us?' OR 'Look at all those stamps and the stickers. Someone be looking out for this bitch and I better play nice!' In this case, to my surprise, it was the latter. Thin crescents lifted as she looked through my little red book a few times. She then returned it, with her engaged hand and smiled like an awkward waitress, handing over a drink she wasn't sure you ordered. I smiled, felt superior for about ten seconds and stepped aside. Perhaps this was the point where I felt changed, but that would be anticlimactic. So, to put it differently: I stepped on the bus, uncertain, unchanged, save for the newly acquired stamps in my passport.

Sedated by smells and the pain in my back, I finally dosed off. I'm not just saying that to wrap this story up neatly. Are you already looking how much till the end? I have a hard time sleeping on buses, so this genuinely happened, because I woke up and the sun was just coming up. And her hair, the woman who is never to become an admirer of my work, was almost golden, instead of cheap, washed out platinum. And her husband was sleeping and I wondered if he dreamt about his dead son. And another woman with her son let him rest his head on her, and felt his warmth against her body. And the woman next to me longed for her daughter. And the deep wrinkles of the old man behind were somehow beautiful, the rugged, tired face of a man who's worked in a field all his life, even though he probably was a mechanic, or sold socks off the hood of a car. Yeah they used to do that where I come from. Not anymore. Because in the not-so-distant future, we became like everyone else. Like you.

This moment of serenity lasted very briefly, before everyone started to wake up slowly. The best I can explain it, is that it feels a little bit like a one-night stand. You've seen them sleep with their mouths open, heard them snore and smelled them in ways you really didn't care to. You feel dirty. Occasionally, like noticing a childhood picture, or a card from his mum, you learn something likeable, even sweet about him. That makes you wonder if it actually could work between you. But then you sober up and realize you will never see him/them again and start putting on your shoes, avoiding eye contact and waiting for the inevitable goodbye. Sixteen hours! That's something, right? If it's a one-night stand, then it's a dinner and movie one, and I sure never had one of those.

Suddenly everyone had someone to call. Call home. I never call, I don't like to talk over the phone, and if there is one thing you take from this, then I really, honestly, and truly hope it's that. Because that's just about the one thing that whoever I am, wherever you find me, whatever I tell you and however you take it-that at least is true. I fucking hate it. So I texted and my mum replied: "Great. We'll be there."

When the bus comes to a halt you don't notice them anymore. You want to leave, you want to *arrive*. Where did I arrive you ask? Maybe I still can't tell you. Maybe I'm moving again. And maybe I'm sitting here, right where you'd expect me to be, ninety-seven percent a woman (my period is late and I told you it's what we think about *a lot*), making up stories to make you think I am the stranger or the hero, or something more than who I am, or might be.

That day though, if you decide to believe me, I did *arrive*, and I saw my mum and dad, who have aged quite a bit, and gotten fatter but still look like my mum and dad. And they were smiling and waving to make sure I'd see them. And then they continue to stare and grin even though they know I saw them. And I did see them, I truly have, but more importantly, as they stood there waving and smiling like a couple of idiots, I saw myself in them. How I was, how I might become but also… how I am. A part of them, as they are a part of me, in some vague concept of somethingness I don't dare name, I could never in no language or words express no matter how marvelous a writer I become. Not a stranger, never a stranger. A daughter. And if you don't believe me and still want to look under my skirt – screw you. I am still a child.

Danica Popovic
Belgrade, Serbia

russian texas

On a made up date in October, I
read the notes on my phone.
You're so
pretty now I notice hips

And cigarettes unraveling
themselves in Texas heat.
Driving west, I watched rabbits
kill themselves in my headlights.

Some believers
wear the feet
around their necks –
a token of death.

A mark of time, when I held
my own hand wishing it was
your jaw. Mayu,
we are not in Maine,

you tell me. Everything plastic
is nasty. I agree.
Familiar like
when I was small.

Running through rows
of potatoes, praying in
Russian to some sun.
Take my light where you love.

                                              Maia Snow
                                              Austin, Texas

tern

                  about how he felt like a shark, which
only dawns on you when he starts mauling your
arm and as serrated teeth fall into your body which
at this point is basically a wound and you think
dimly, the thoughts of an anomalocaris or a cave fish
which never has eyes, that something bad is happening
out underneath the aching gray patterns of a
Days Inn hallway, in a field, in a marriage bed,
and the springs creak as he tears out your
entrails, he kisses your liver before swallowing
it whole. your underwear had hearts on it
because it was the same material as the
ironing board you stole from a Holiday Inn. your
lover is- hungry you are hungry but you can no
longer stomach the thought of food. you come
to on a mattress in the Hilton and the cotton
around you has stained red, you
look out the window and the highway is
empty.

                                      Nathan Rivera Mindt
                                            United States

this house is a time capsule

The outside world has changed, but Spring Street remains. This beige shingled house is at the top of a hill, sheltered from the city where modernity is rampant, like a plague. Standing up here, behind a chainlink fence with a sign that says, "please shut the gate", one can easily see the mirage of housewives returning from the market, their wood paneled trim station wagons neatly pulled into their carports. They open their doors with the neat line of tiny triangle windows, carrying in paper bags of fresh produce. This the land of beehive hairdos, kitten heels, and champagne glasses filled to the brim. A flag waves against a Mary blue sky and pastel dresses twirl like a lyrical symbol of domestic bliss. Here, in the teal tiled bathrooms, hair curlers and false eyelashes create eternal, ageless beauty. Saddle shoes at the end of chubby baby-soft legs dash up the pavement and striped shirts pass in a dizzying flash, racing to play in the plot of land that serves as a de facto baseball field, army base, and exotic jungle. Summers are sweet like buttercream and banana splits. Lawn mowers drone in the lazy humidity - starting in June and continuing on until the yellow buses roll up the hill again. Soon September rolls around and the freshly installed air conditioners whir on and souvenirs from a vacation to the beach are lined up on a child's wooden shelf. It is, at last, the dreaded season when the schoolchildren must leave behind their endless hours of daylight and dancing, and return to the classrooms whose air is still permeated green from the hue of trees standing just outside the windows. But the happiness doesn't disappear like smoke from the last bonfire of the summer. It stays, even as another year goes by and more boys grow 7 inches in as many months and more girls give their hearts away. White communion dresses turn to white wedding cakes and the wheel of life turns once more.

Still, here on Spring Street, there is a clean garden of kitsch - plastic pink flamingos, a chainlink fence and a clear blue swimming pool, hydrangea and blades of serpentine green grass, wind chimes that seem to ring even when there is not a wind to be seen or felt. This is not a crowded, clumpy display of garbage and laziness. It is the last man standing in a graveyard of the ever changing trends, cars, and mindsets that pass through like violent thunderstorms. It is a testament to the truth of living honestly and consistently.

Every star spangled childhood summer was spent here. Green carpet, dripping wet hair, air conditioner goosebumps, and the shed with all the tools & pool toys that always felt 20 degrees warmer than the outside and smelled like the air was bathed in chlorine. Even in the deepest, darkest part of winter, I can still feel the shock of the cold bathroom floor beneath feet that might as well have turned into a mermaid tail from diving and floating beneath the sweltering sun. Somewhere in the distance, fireworks whistle and crack in the endless sea of sky.

Day after day, splashing in the rippling pool water, savoring sandwiches on white bread and ice cold cans of soda- the beads of water rolling down the sides like the mascara inked tears of a secretary in a slip dress knowing that the man will never commit to leaving his wife.

As the sky darkens and dusk passes to black, the deck light turns on and buzzes as moths float around. We return to the water after we spent an hour insisting we wanted to go home. Rosaries are passed around and the night remains warm, the crickets begin to sing, and the stars twinkle.

It is painful when I think of these days of my childhood, and days even further down the road of dusty snapshots that I flip through endlessly, knowing there is no tangible return to this. Still, in the depths of my longing for those endless red, white, & blue heat waves, I am aware that the air on Spring Street defies time. It is an airy homecoming to what has been lost to the passage of generations who pledge to do better than their predecessors.

There are ghosts on Spring Street now, but they're fragile like lace from a distant land that no longer exists, and perhaps never did. From even the lightest of touches, they disintegrate and dissipate into the beams of sunlight, like dust motes. But when the light catches just right, they are close enough to see clearly, and sometimes hear, as they go about their days, unaware of what happens around them, as a girl from the 21st century studies their technicolor outlines and tries to reconcile this life so many light years from them.

Madeline Mecca
Upstate New York, United States

going no where

Several weeks ago the house flooded. Needless to say, I have become displaced. Insurance put me up at this hotel. I haven't been home in weeks, and believe it or not, under these circumstances, I would rather be back in West Covina, a suburb of Los Angeles where the American Dream is suspended in a white fog- a slow, enduring euthanasia.

It's not a tall hotel but it's big. The Shilo Inn is four stories but has halls that wrap around the entire weed wrecked hill. To the west, there's what could have been a nice view. Instead, the trademark ornaments of abandoned industry litter the train tracks that run along the heel of the hill to which the Shilo Inn has been assigned and forgotten.

It's very late, and I've had very little sleep. Still, though, I'm awake. I am sitting at a window overlooking the East San Gabriel Valley in the early morning and the only light is that which is provided by street lamps, where the rest is darkness in the palm of this dry, withered valley.

The darkness closes its fist, and it's late or early and I cannot sleep.

The hotel is a body, and like a body it has many veins, except its veins have run dry. It's mostly dead. All that's left are neglected carpet and peeling wall paper. They still replace the small bars of soap and bottles of shampoo, but there is no one here to use them. The place is empty and decrepit, and the more I am here, the more I am as well. I feel the blood become like sand, and the arteries like vast deserts. The only thing that keeps anything moving now is the wind; I hear it beat against the palms of the tree below my window. Besides that, there is only the echo of my own existence slipping off the walls. Whatever I'm doing here becomes less and less like living and more like the cold residence of an obvious void, a tomb.

Since I have been here, up until recently, I haven't seen anyone else. At times, while walking along the long hall to my room, I have heard voices behind a door, but they are faint and hardly there. They are like shadows to me- shadows that do not have bodies. I leave the TV running, not watching but listening to the voices like they are there, like they are people in the room and I know them, but I don't want to bother with their conversation, and I am amused, not distraught. Shadows that I assume have a shape of origin and the courtesy of warm, moving blood.

A few days ago I encountered another resident. We both looked at each other as though the other did not belong here- as if we were fighting over this particular hell, and for whatever reason it had become comfortable enough for us, alone, but not enough to share- not at all.

She was an overweight middle aged woman. I was in the lobby and it wasn't too late yet and I know this because I had just made my way from the liquor store, and the store closed before eleven in the pm every night. I pressed the button for the elevator and waited. It was then she approached, all whatever hundreds of pounds of her, stinking through her too small, struggling clothes. She stood next to me and looked ahead toward the closed elevator door as though she expected some kind of revelation, something more than the arrival of the elevator that might reveal to her the solution to all of her life's troubles.

"Never seen you here before," she said. "I've been here a week. No one here before that."

Still, even when addressing me, her eyes were fixed ahead. There was some distant hope for her maybe. I wanted to believe she saw it and wasn't letting go.

"I've been here, actually," I said, "the past month or so…"

She said nothing, and she kept her eyes fixed. Not even a nod from this woman, and that was okay with me. I had nothing else to say just then and really nothing even before that.

When the elevator finally arrived I was still wishing her well, imagining that perhaps not too long ago she wasn't so wasted away- that she, like me, had at some point enjoyed moments in the sun that could not have possibly been torn from their fabric. Because as a girl her parents moved her out west from some bible belt town, and it was a difficult move, but all that didn't matter when they took her to see the ocean for the first time, and it was big and forever looking, and so was her future, and then, at that time, it was something to dance in.

She stepped into the elevator and the doors closed. I watched them close and her eyes as they closed before her, still fixed at some point, and I hoped that it was that day at the beach she was so intent on not losing.

I let the elevator leave without me. I took the stairs, and the room was clean- the bed made and fresh when I arrived.

I've decided that I might as well stay awake for the continental breakfast.

To be honest, I've had better breakfast at the Los Angeles county jail. There are pancakes, but they're cold, even at 6 AM when you'd assume they'd be fresh. The last time I went down for breakfast I decided that I might as well toast the pancake, but then it became stiff and impossible to eat.

The breakfast begins at 6 in the am. It's almost that time, and though I'm not really hungry, it feels like a normal enough thing to do. And as I do, I remember the old man from yesterday morning.

It was yesterday morning at breakfast.

No words were exchanged, just expressions. And really the only reason we even ended up at the same place was that I stuck around for maybe an hour expecting more, better food. The sun began to shine through the lobby. The dining area was adjacent to a large window through which the hills of Pomona concealed the rising sun. As the minutes passed, the room became brighter, gradually cutting out the shape and color of the hills in light. In the darkness it was easy to accept I was alone, but now it was clear that someone else was there with me.

The man was alone and more alone than me, even though no one else was there.

While I didn't feel that he was very old, his face looked as though it had endured centuries of erosion- something I'd expect from a canyon, grand or not. Nothing he was wearing was less than a decade old. I assumed he was a trucker, but I knew he wasn't there on business. His expression was troubled- some kind of cocktail: a mix of anger, regret and purpose.

He drank coffee, and he was drinking it black. Though our eyes never crossed and he never gave me his attention, I felt his plight, and it burrowed deep and shook, shivering in the cold light of the early morning.

It all became very clear to me:

The man isn't here for work. It's his daughter's wedding, and he wasn't invited. It seems that she made no attempt to conceal the fact, that she wanted him to know it was happening and wanted him to know that he wasn't welcome, that he wouldn't be walking her down the aisle. I could see he didn't disagree with her. He was angry, but not at her.

The man sipped the black coffee and didn't grimace at the terrible taste. It was, after all, recycled from yesterday's breakfast. He was stoic but not proud in that lobby at the table in the early morning light. In his room, laid out across the bed was a second hand suit, his best at the moment, and he was thinking about the look on her face when he arrived, and hoped that she would at least allow him to stand at the back of the church during the ceremony and was assuring himself that even that would be some sort of victory.

I looked at him some more before I realized that I was actually staring, not that he cared or even really noticed me. It was, however, enough for me to get the hint. I got up from the table, pocketing the last hardboiled egg.

At 6 in the morning in the lobby the sun hasn't risen yet. At this time of year it comes closer to seven, but I can already make out that the darkness is becoming more of a purple. I'm not so much exhausted but really just tired of being awake and thinking what I've been thinking, thinking about the overweight woman and the old man, that really maybe whatever story I conjured up for them was much less tragic than what actually is, or that I'm making them more interesting than they are, or that perhaps some people were just born in a place and walked in a straight line from that place and ended up where they ended up with no dreams or regrets to have, even from the beginning.

These days the rising sun is a sure sign I should get some sleep. I'm here at breakfast and it's the same pancakes and nothing else besides stale cereal. No one is here, not the woman or the man. I expect to be alone this morning and I'll return to my bed the same way.

David Duenas
San Gabriel Valley, Los Angeles

heat

When it's a bouncing baby boy, he will grow to form a full strong man,   But when it's a beautiful baby girl, she will grow because she just has to grow.
               She will outgrow her princess ways to trace tracks back to her mother's rage,   she will relive her pain. She will live backwards
          she will crawl back to take the shape of her mother's fury.   She will learn to burn, you will misread her breathing, but never miss her smoke.   She will evaporate the water held by her eyes and the salt will burn her insides until   she learns to smile when she cries.
                    she will grow because she just has to grow, but not into the son that I need.
     Father, I never meant to burn you, you were too cold to be alive   I just wanted to be the sun that you needed,
          the light you needed to escape your darkness,
                         but I never knew that dark was I.
          The only resemblance left for a baby girl to inherit was your artistic measures,   I only grew back to your knuckles,
          held my head high aimed at your canvas imprinting art for the world   to ignore claiming she is just a growing baby girl and what does she know?
So forgive me father for your sons know not what they do
                    and they know not what to do,
          so what they do is them trying to show you what not to do,
                    because semen is kept to be trapped in bottles labeled female
                    subjected to regenerate the echoes left by our fathers,
   to keep the candle of hope burning for our mothers
                    until the candle wax burns off
          and the rope connects with our intestines

and we keep burning ourselves. Creating eternal internal warmth for the sons we are yet to carry yet when they inherit their mother's heat they do not know how to handle it so exerts it on our skin with a slap on the face and still carry the audacity to complain of us being burnt. Well are we not castles, we are bricks to standing castles, our hearts the fireplace. Are we not breaking gracefully onto our own hands and are you not amazed by how we carry ourselves? So yes, it is a beautiful baby girl and she will grow to be a strong because she twists, she turns and curls, she holds her volcano with stillness compressing and suppressing all of her lava so do no dare anger her Gods. Her being girl was just an attempt of being a cape less superhero, because father I tried to save you. When mothers bare suns for father's they can not stand the heat of another man's flame

Mvula Thee Rain (Nomvula Zobuhle Ngcobo)
Pietermaritzburg, KwaZulu-Natal, South Africa

in march we fell in love

The ground is wet and filled with robins.
The trees are bare and waiting for spring.
The birds are looking for food and happy.
The air is singing

                      a song of everything.

The sun is hiding in blankets of clouds.
The moon is asleep and dreaming.
The stars are always there.
Whether or not

                      they are seen.

My past is the fertile ground for the present.
My body is waking to its own full love.
My belly is where I find my feelings.
My heart is singing

                      in praise of being.

There is dew on the grass.
The ground is open.
Lightning comes down to ignite our steps.
It shines on the empty places where we

                      come out.

                      Cassie Premo Steele, Ph.D.
                      Columbia, SC, USA

the amorous arab

It is Monday.
The Austrian German teacher is a she.
The Austrian German teacher slips of the
tongue.
she gives homework.
The Austrian German teacher slips of the
pen/attaches
spelling mistakes to a large board
with a smooth and dark surface
attached to the wall.
The amorous Arab notes down the words
right-writing-errors.
his teacher is so beautiful that we (we?)
feel like bursting.
We (we?) speak of rapid combustions.
Ask: "Decompositions?"
And demand excessive internal pressures.
she speaks:
i want you to write/to pen/
to put down a summary
of your last summer holidays.
Describe a certain event,
describe an exciting experience.
something, you made for enjoyment,
amusement
and lighthearted pleasure, fun.
Prove playful behavior/good humor,
you know? Maybe a
festival, feast day,
féte, fiesta,
celebration, anniversary,
jubilee, or a trip,
tour, journey, voyage?
no furlough,
no sabbatical,
but getaway,
sojourn.
Write down, she says,
write down what i wrote down;
write down sojourn.

And below: stay, visit, stop, stopover,
vacation.
learn!
Acquire a knowledge of the German language,
acquire skill in being German.
Become competent in behaving like me,
grasp, master, take in, absorb, digest,
assimilate,
familiarize yourself with
the homework.
The amorous Arab is motivated:
hm, let me gather, understand, ascertain,
establish, (then learn by heart, commit
to memory).
The amorous (but imperfect and un-German
and uncultured and poorly educated and
quasi-illiterate) Arab feels
motivated as he wants to write a summary
about how he met the Pervert Persian and
the Juser-friendly Jew, and why he's
given them these names, and why
Jew's surname is
Juser-friendly and not
user-friendly.
Quickly and unexpectedly: he recalls how
he came face to face with Death
last summer and decides to write
about that.
The Austrian German teacher
collects the texts one week later.
The Austrian German teacher
piles them up on her desk.
she articulates and pronounces the
following almost perfectly:
"Arrgh, you know, i don't feel so well.
i feel dizzy the whole day already.
Write down:
giddy, lightheaded,
faint, unsteady,
shaky, muzzy.
i've got a headache and probably fever.
headache not in the sense of:
trouble, problem,

bother, bugbear,
vexation, irritation.
But in the sense of
pain in the head,
migraine, neuralgia.
in addition to that i feel a nausea coming
up and wouldn't it be embarrassing to
run to the toilet in the middle of my
own lesson? And imagine the
bathroom would be occupied at
that very
moment.
Then i would have to vomit right in the
hallway.
And i would have to throw up into my hands.
What a nightmare. no. That's not gonna
happen.
Therefore, i suggest that we finish
today's lessons right now.
Alright?
The schoolmaster will certainly
permit it. so don't worry about that.
see you next week."
The amorous Arab fills his bag, esp. with
items needed when away from home.
he says partly Tschüss, partly good-bye,
to his schoolmates and steps into the
external side of school called
real
life.
Both feet of the amorous Arab hurt.
The amorous Arab is proud of not
feeling
pain.
A coincidence outside:
when passing a famous black man
(of more than average height)
the amorous one bows down.
And he thinks:
a star!
At Monday evening he does recall his way
back home.
he uses verbs (esp. verbs/many verbs) in

his head.
The thoughts (alphabetically):
absorb,
admit,
affect,
analyze,
annoy,
apologize,
argue,
attack,
baptize,
bedim,
censor,
ignore,
insult,
pay,
provoke,
thank,
torch,
undress,
undo.
let me answer the question
Why does he think so?
by recalling the events that happened
on the way back home from
the lesson.
of course:
A feeling of discomfort and weakness
caused by lack of food,
coupled with the desire to eat,
after the language course.
in this shop,
this two-euro-fifty-meal
(of highest quality/first class)
warmed up by Kurds; it had been
sticky and sultry.
i mean: the climate.
The amorous one had sweated and
thought literally:
isweatmyselfhalfdead (one word).
he had sweated himself half dead and had
taken his T-shirt off in the name of
Allah.

(The T-shirt.
This shirt.
What a T-shirt...)
he has been
gazed at, and stared at, like gaped at,
almost peered at, my god, peeped at:
beglotzt.
never in my life have i been looked at
like that.
That's on the one hand disgusting, but on
the other hand it is certainly a kind of
attention.
And attention isn't a bad thing in itself.
look, attention
is consideration
is contemplation
is deliberation
is thought
is study
is observation
is scrutiny
is investigation means action.
someone insults me.
Many insult me.
What a scornful abuse.
What a disrespectful behaviour.
how
Kurdish.
he had been insulted, but he had also
threatened/threatened/threatened back
by speaking:
oh, you practitioners of complementary
medicine, you mystics, you spirituals.
oh, notice the emanation surrounding my
body, look at my T-shirt that's lying
in your shop's corner.

Sina Khani
Berlin, Germany

eels

Oneirologists, you're out of line!
out of work, out of fashion
pack up your electrodes and your readouts
get to the nearest bus station, and ride the dusty road out of town
We're taking back our dreams

My friend had a dream about me—
do you know what it is for someone to tell you their dream of you?
My house was filled with water
on purpose, she tells me
and there were eels everywhere
"They jumped out of the water and bit my earrings!"
The dream, a poem
one only she could bring forth
it cannot be reduced
(do not dare to reduce my eels!)

Do you know what it is to dream of someone?
Ah, pour out what's in the beakers
come to my balcony
There I'll treat you to the humid air and the ever-changing clouds
There we'll drink, and spin, and know nothing

                         Mollie Swayne
                    Tennessee, United States

let me quit. now. (please?)

As per the trajectory of most self-indulgent children, I always felt perfectly adequate as a disappointment to others. If you're staring into the face of failure, congratulations, you're one step ahead. Quit before failure and your defeat transforms into a memory where ignorance grants you the hindsight of a pleasant and rewarding experience. I highly recommend this tactic, bolstered by years of experience. For example, at the wise age of 5 I begged incessantly for guitar lessons. I spent a month playing what could only be vaguely recognized as the Shrek soundtrack, before deciding that my hands were too small and putting the guitar down forever -- a young age to relinquish my dreams of rock stardom. At seven, I heroically stepped down from my place at the piano, as it seemed like that was more of my sister's calling.

I started voice lessons for a brief stint and spent an hour a week belting grating chords with the school voice teacher. Pam was round and happy, and she gave me stickers as a reward for time I spent practicing at home. Between the ages of seven and fourteen I would do practically anything for a sticker (I really wish I could lie about this) so, it seemed like the voice lessons would continue. Cursed luck on the dreams of my parents! My sister took voice lessons too and it was soon evident that while she was moving on to sing Adele and Ella Fitzgerald, I was still stuck on the Winnie the Pooh theme song. Tragic to lay my pipes to rest so soon but, again, heroic in the name of sibling pride. Fifth grade was the year of the saxophone, which nobody enjoyed. My tiny hands (think raccoon sized) could not reach the high D and for this, I quickly fell behind my sister in terms of musical clout. There was talk of her training to one day audition for American Idol. I, on the other hand, garnered praise (and nausea) from the sheer amount of ramen I could consume in one Saturday afternoon.

"Anya…did you finish all the ramen already?" The tone: shock and disgust.

"Yeah. Do we have any Cheetos?" The tone: feigned ignorance to the situation at hand.

Aside from my incredibly humble and empathetic personality, being the less talented sibling did come with drawbacks. For instance, nobody noticed that I was not physically in shape at all and they continued to make me participate on a local Rec soccer team every Spring. My dad was a volunteer coach. I had never disliked my dad before this. Sure, he liked sports and "working hard," but other than that he was my best friend.

In seventh grade, I begged my parents to let me quit. I whined. I pleaded. So, I was shocked to discover that both of them were in agreement that I finish the season because I had "made commitments" and it "wouldn't be fair" to my dad who had only become my coach to "spend quality time with me." Disgusting. His prowess on the soccer field did not transfer to his ramen loving, saxophone hating, Winnie the Pooh singing youngest daughter. The only good part about Rec soccer was that after the game I was allowed to buy both a hot dog and a family sized pack of M&Ms.

Each year at the end of the season, the coaches had to rate their players that the teams for the next season would be based on. Nobody ever rated lower than B-. That year, I caught a glimpse of my dad's clipboard to find that he had rated me a B. As a student of a small, progressive school, this was the first real grade I ever received. When you're evaluated your entire life on the "could improve, satisfactory, excellent" scale, a B feels like a passive reprimand for stupidity. Betrayal! By my own father.

While Saturdays were becoming my least favorite day of the week because of mandatory hellish sports, I looked upon Sundays favorably as the day my dad took my sister and I to our favorite candy store. This was a tradition that began when we were little, and as we got older it became harder to convince our dad to make the trip every week. Re: the sticker obsession, my childhood habits died a slow and agonizing death.

One particular Sunday, my dad agreed to take us to the candy store if we stopped by the soccer fields on the way. I was suspicious as to his intentions, but the promise of chocolate covered gummy bears trumps all logic. We arrived at the empty soccer field in my dad's pick-up truck. I sat in the middle seat that was mistakenly designed to be concave up. My sister hopped out of her side of the truck and my dad began rummaging in the back for a soccer ball.

"What're you doing?" I demanded. I did not get out.

"Oh, come on." My dad rolled his eyes. "We'll just kick the ball around a little bit and then we can get candy."

My sister and him began passing the ball back and forth. I whined. I pleaded. I stomped the dashboard with my dirty shoes. This was a cruel joke. Trickery! My own father—a backstabber! He ignored my cries of injustice. I got out of the truck so he could hear me more clearly.

"Don't close that door." He shouted. "The keys are in there!"

I pretended not to hear. I gave him what I considered to be my most spiteful glare, and slammed the door shut.

"Are you serious." He yelled as he ran over. The door was locked, the phone and the keys were in the car. There was no one else at the soccer field. We were surrounded by a wooded highway. My outrage bubbled into immediate guilt.

"Im sooorrrrryyyyy!" The tone: I still blame you for this entire situation.

"Goddamnit." The tone: my daughter is an effing brat.

The nearest public phone was a half mile walk on the side of the highway. To someone who had been promised a joyous afternoon of gummy bears and sitting still, this was equivalent to running a half marathon. My dad laughed, already aware of the injustice I felt. My contempt for my least favorite sport was met with a vicious karma.

The entire walk I tried to make up for my snotty behavior.

Me: "Wow at least now we can see how big the road signs are, up close!"

My sister: "Shut up."

As an adult, I think now that I might have slapped my younger self. But my dad was lighthearted and, I like to think, in debt to me for the B rating. My mom eventually came and brought us the spare keys. She and my dad amused themselves at my expense, forever searing the day into my brain as a humiliating set back. This is a parenting technique I now recognize and respect. We made it home, but I don't remember if we ever got the candy.

The next week, I started drum lessons.

Anya Ptacek
St Paul, MN

how to miss a place you've never visited

my grandmothers fed me rice from their weathered hands when i was little
basmati in one house, jasmine in the other
yoga and prayer mats and alhamdulillah on saturday
dried mango and fried banana and talk of maria magdalena on sunday

i used to count to myself in tagalog
isa, dalawa, tatlo, apat
bragged when i learned how to say shoes in arabic,
like saying the words would bring me closer to something
like beckoning someone for dinner with a phrase i could speak but not spell
like grasping at the meanings of sentences with a few familiar words

i don't know how to tell you where i'm from;
i've been from feudal china, from ancient greece, from the western frontier
i've been from 7,641 islands i can't picture
i've been from the unnamed village in a scary story about curses and djinn,
i can tell you my lola is from manila
my nana is from singapore
my dad is from florida
and my mom is from halfway between asia and the east coast
and i wish i could be a good malaysian
and i wish i could be a good filipino
but i was supposed to be american;
american means not knowing who my ancestors were for the first decade of my life
american means i was raised on oatmeal until i asked for pancit
american means being denied my birthright,
being the only one in the family who speaks one language

i'm not from texas the way my cousins are
i'm not from new york the way my friends are
i'm not from asia the way my family is
i couldn't tell you where i'm from in such small terms.
i'm from a hot kitchen that smells like adobo at night,

i'm from a garden by the train tracks that grows persimmon and kumquat and lemongrass,
i'm from a doorway with two wicker fans hanging off the panels.
in my name are the saints of two different faiths
and i am from all of those places and more.

we convene over rice at every family gathering—
that never changes.
my ancestors ate it in wooden houses by the sea,
we had it in texas on a long glass table,
in new york in a kitchen that's three feet wide
my legs crossed on the chair
ankle on calf, an edited meditation pose
ask me if it hurts.
the truth is, it's gentler

> Lex Mohamed
> Astoria, NY, USA

ER coup d'état

Alone in a land only days away from martial law &
mandatory curfew, half my face
fell suddenly numb. No pins, no
hatching of a thousand crickets
down the skin.
It just gave up, hardened & resolute
as a man released from prison.

I chewed street breakfast
with the other side of my mouth &
went looking for a hospital.

*

Lumphini Park was dotted with flowers &
urgency & plastic tents &
pamphlets in English for journalists.
Over tea & music I scribbled useless notes.

This story has been written,
rearranged, bled out & revised too many times.
Homemade signs in the universal language of protest.

The police & food carts & generals & wide-brimmed hats
& owners of industry & hawkers
mix in Bangkok streets with buses & cabs &
motorbikes with helmetless passengers
like giant traffic circles
everyone going round
avoiding each other
until they can't.

*

I was given a plastic bracelet &
a carton of water.
Forgetting,
it poured out the side of my mouth.
Between x-rays I repeated this
for a laugh in the bathroom mirror.

Demurring on the molar extraction but
settling on penicillin,
I kept the bill as a souvenir.

*

At a restaurant with a slim pier on the Chao Phraya
I drank Chang in bottles.
The breeze felt like a travel novel.
At this time of day in New York
those with rooftop coups release pigeons &
let them fly.

Famously painted on a shop gate on Khaosan road:
NATION OF SHEEP
RULED BY WOLVES
OWNED BY PIGS

If you wish to escape,
chase injustice.

*

Retreated to the room
-the cost of a cup of coffee-
a single bulb, a cot &
a blanket as meagre as a threadbare marriage.

A beetle flints around
red sheen in the streetlight
it's bombinating paused only by the pane
that won't give way.

It lands &
searches the glass for cracks.

Craig Chisholm
Bangkok

the twelfth station (XII)

It was written and it has been told,
That even as she watched her son die, pale body hanging
Limp from a tree like some other, much luckier, mother's laundry
She said nothing and instead looked up at him with sweet, damp eyes
And cried quietly into the soft fabric of her sleeve.

Softly, too is how the blood oozed from his bludgeoned flesh
And trickled to the ground, the river of copper- scented red
Mingling with the coarse sand below how some rowdy group of teenagers might,
At the beach, or in one of those gaudily lit shopping malls.

The bright lights of screens and shop windows prove too much or not enough,
And they prowl the place for warm blood to spill on the sand,
Or dirty pavement with chewing gum stamped in
To feel less like the grimy footpath and a little more alive.
Funny, those lines between life and death and boredom, and how men would rather
Searing pain of war and suffering than the cool breeze on their cheeks of nothing at all.

There was a boy I knew who wanted pain so badly that one winter,
He stole his friend's car, crashed it straight into a tree so spectacularly
He splintered the bark and crushed the engine along with a little bit of his head.
Perhaps the injury was still not enough pain for the boy,
Or maybe he wanted to emulate that other, perfect son hanging from a tree,
But he pulled his belt from around his waist, wrapped one end around his neck,
The other around a branch of the oak he had done battle with- and swung.

A catastrophe of boy and belt and wood and metal,
The corpse was nothing when laid beside his mother's cudgelled heart,
An organ so mangled it was truly a miracle the woman could still stand at all,
And did not become a scrumpled thing strewn across the bones of her son.
Funny too, that she will deem the fact she can still get dressed in the morning

And open a box of Raisin Bran and swallow instead of letting her eyes, sore from crying,
Wet her pillow like a cat's piss wets everything it can- A miracle.

It is a blessing from God that she finds the strength to go on,
Slowly though, so not to irritate those lacerations cross her heart,
Yet still they burn as though she'd pressed a shroud of saltwater to them,
That saltwater found in a vast ocean, the one she likes to visit
When she's done with the graveyard-
To breathe in the stinging air and remind herself she is still alive.

And sometimes I too look out at the sea or up at that dark sky full of empty stars
And wonder why some young boys are so desperate to bleed and die, and if
I'll be able to look at oak trees again and not see a crucifix.
And just like that, life goes on for those who can stomach it
And those who can stomach getting hurt by those who cannot.

> Maria Harkin
> Belfast, Northern Ireland

coffee shop sonder

Winter rain and I'm sat with a cardboard cup
coffee ahead of me followed by the window
looking at the people passing on the cobbles
to the Georgian stations waiting trains.
No ticking wristwatch strapped to my skin
so I stop to see the nameless faces
piggy-backing electric rucksacks,
dragging bursting wheeled suitcases.

All detached from the wet strangers
till you walked by and gave a tight half-smile.
A week passed since we cried goodbye
and I aimed to push you to the league of strangers
for our connection can rub clean
with your face joining the masses - never nameless,
but then nobody is without a name.
As you passed from sight to a new life

the window showed me names I'd missed,
faces un-blurred and knife-edged sharpened
names made their journey home and to workplaces
and fleshed out thousands of crisp letters
all with a digital fingerprint and login details
to store their swelling wishes and families,
friends and likes, verified and subscribed
seeing their physical fingerprints through the rain.

Interwoven netted lives are darned together
to replace holes left by ripped and broken ties
stretched too far, to the hundreds, in high-tech ages
of fast stitching and faster seam ripping.
Hours spill from my unstitched pockets
and if you weren't the hole I'd have called it lost time.
Named complexities walk the streets every day
but we block them out to make space for ourselves.

Carl Lewis Griffin
Newcastle Upon Tyne

feng shui

For years we had a crystal tortoise in a crystal tray filled with water near the front door. Dad had picked it up during a hill station trip, intrigued by the notion of 'feng shui.' We first heard of the term sometime during our adolescence, when the weekly market was flooded with bamboo plants and Laughing Buddhas and Chinese coins and chimes. They stood for prosperity, longevity, stability and so on: at their core, for money and affluence. So one day, when Dad got to know that exotic turtles were being sold in lower-town market, he rushed to buy a pair. He brought them home, tiny coin-sized creatures with golden-moss-green shells, placed them on the teapoy and said: for our Home Sweet Home! We brothers were mildly excited; although Mom frowned and mumbled about how Dad incessantly occupied himself with superstitious rituals to multiply his meagre income so that he could buy a new sofa and repair the old geyser and think of a new bike. She threw out the bundle of yellow plastic flowers that was tied in the north corner of their bedroom the previous week to usher in marital happiness. Mom boiled him a cup of tea and, wiping the sweat off her forehead, picked one of those turtles up on her palm. It bobbed its neck up and down and then pulled itself inside the shell, all but the conical tail. Mom smiled and ran her fingers across the etched shell. It twitched.

Turtle Food was bought, which smelt the ugliest smell of earthworm and seafood and discarded remains of meat. We watched videos of turtles eating watermelons and cabbage leaves and harassed ours to consume those, but they wouldn't. They loved the Turtle Food. They were kept in a plastic tub with a raised flat stone in the centre of it, so that they could swim and bask as it pleased them. Only months later when they grew up to a palm-size were they allowed to roam the house and hide under furniture and crawl over the carpet.

Mom had become accustomed to the routine of feeding them, scrubbing their shells with an old toothbrush, and talking her sweet somethings to them. We were out for our trades by then and visited our parents over the weekends and saw her ritually involved with the pets. Dad would scroll his phone screen all day long, as the turtles crawled everywhere and came to rest on Mom's feet, one on each foot. Lounging themselves there, they pulled in their legs, shut their eyelids and froze in their relaxed position. She would sit still for hours, letting the turtles nap, losing herself in a world of crawling thoughts.

During summers the turtles could roam around the house and fix a spot of their choosing at night. One morning, when Mom went looking for them after breakfast, she was horrified to find the brown one under the shoe rack on the balcony. There were blood spots all over the place. She went on her knees and pulled it out with a stick. It was bitten badly. Its nails on all four limbs were gone, the tail had almost disappeared and the tip of the mouth was chomped too. It was attacked in the night, perhaps all throughout the night. Mom felt guilty that she had postponed feeding them that day, having no idea how long the poor thing was wreathing in blood and pain. She felt deep pity for the mute fellow. Dad wasn't around. She cleaned the blood with a cotton swab, her cheeks hot with tears, consoling the pet in her soft soothing voice, speaking to it of the horrible night. It was easily deduced that the culprits must have been mice from the debris of an under-construction villa in the neighborhood. The rodents would have climbed up the sewage pipes at night to prey upon the turtle.

In a few days, Brownie had given up on its Turtle Food, did not move around much and had developed a fungal infection. Dad casually remarked that turtles could carry infectious germs and it was best to lay the poor thing off in the river. Mom screamed at him for his cold cruelty and asked him to shove his rationality up his. Dad was quiet, for a change, and did not retaliate or threaten. He was beginning to feel ashamed of his words when I offered it to be taken to the municipal vet. I did, got it injected with a brown fluid, and bought a liquid food solution that was to be fed orally twice a day. Mom would sit for half an hour, morning and evening, Brownie in her lap trying to feed it with a glass dropper. She spoke to it as gently as usual and tried comforting it with her words. The other turtle, Goldie, would stick himself up her toe and wait for his turn to be petted.

One afternoon the week of the mice-attack, Mom had visited one of our neighbors and procured their old mousetrap. It was an antique thing made of a copper frame- a cuboidal wired box with a tiny gate that could be suspended with a nail, as the bait was placed halfway through its entrance. Rat poison was also bought and kept strategically at various places across the balcony, on windowsills, and in hidden corners of the house. Two days later we woke up to a not-fully-grown mouse squealing around inside the trap cage.

Brownie was in a bad condition, its limbs amputated, couldn't budge from where it was placed. I saw Mom after feeding it, took it close to the mouse trap and spoke in her baby-voice: Is this the demon who hurt you? Was it the gang that troubled you all night as I snored out my dreams?... And then very calmly, she lifted out the flat stone from the turtle's tub, half-filled with water, and placed the mousetrap inside it. The mouse screeched and yelped as it drowned; I walked away, Dad perhaps tried saying something but was met with Mom's narrow eyes. The balcony door was latched and the mouse was left to die. The screaming stopped a while later and the trap was emptied into the dustbin, coolly.

The average life span of a domesticated Red-eared Turtle is about 25 years. Brownie, after showing initial signs of recovery, died in a few months with some form of internal infectious growth. Mom didn't smile for a long time and it led to a perpetual sunken mood across the household. Dad was mostly preoccupied with his phone. It was incomprehensible to Mom how someone could be so interested in the Prime Minister's speech on hazards of open defecation and completely blind to the sorrows of his neighbours or the tears of his own wife.

Beyond feng shui, Dad seemed to be exploring the rich indigenous heritage of totems and rituals towards spiritual and material upliftment. When one of his office colleagues visited one evening for tea, he was informed about Brownie and the eventual death. After a moment's pause, the gentleman remarked, of course citing an authentic anecdote of an unverifiable person from his ancestral village, that a turtle's shell was the most auspicious of things concerning the Goddess of Wealth. Upon deliberation, we were informed that the ritual had its roots in a primitive culture around his coastal village. A turtle's shell, hollowed out and inverted, should be filled with sesame oil and be fitted with a wick and lit as a lamp on a no-moon night at the base of a fig tree: the results could be never-heard-of wonders and fortunes of sudden riches.

And that which was a worthless shell was dug out from under the garden soil by Dad. Brownie had been buried about a week ago. The white flowers on its top had barely decomposed, its own body was almost intact. Mom kept herself away from this foolish business, wallowing in her weakness at not being able to protect a voiceless thing from a pathetic death. Goldie, too had started looking solitary in its tub-pond and didn't swim much, sat himself on the rock and slept the days away.

I saw Dad fill the pit with two packets of salt and place the turtle's body back in its grave. He didn't bother to replace the flowers. The salt, it seemed, was meant to fasten the disintegration. The next month, a day before the no-moon, Dad dug the pit and removed the shell. He washed it and cleaned it with a brush, inside and out, and left it to dry on the veranda. I saw Mom standing quietly and watching; she did not touch it. Bathed in afternoon sun, the shell looked like a relic from a distant past and the gaping hollows made me feel miserable. Mom did not speak her sweet somethings to Goldie either. She never smiled except when we customarily complimented her cooking during our weekend lunches, and that too, a forlorn distant smile, like a blunt-creased origami fold.

Later that year, the eldest of us brought home the good news of having been selected for a multinational company that offered him a monthly salary equivalent to Dad's half-yearly income.

Dad was proud and he rang up all our relatives with the news. The following year my younger brother did unexpectedly well with his new business of tiling materials, and our family found itself rich beyond local comprehension. Dad got himself a costly phone and a costly earphone and continued with his costly-things-to-order-online and took to renovation and so on. Mom was bought colorful dresses of nobody's choice in handcrafted silk and was surprised with jewelry and the like. There was no investment and only the spending of money, like we had always dreamt of doing.

We hosted a big party for everyone we knew and told them we were celebrating Life itself and, when people asked why, we said that there was no reason not to. Mom spoke to people, but everybody noticed that she didn't laugh. And that festive night, after everyone had eaten and left, Dad screamed out his lungs at Mom leaping up from the new sofa. He declared that his wife's despair was the sole reason for our constant inauspiciousness all these years. How could the Goddess of Wealth be pleased if the lady of the household gave no damn to her ways and kept crying and whining and weeping over casual matters! Dad in his rage said that Mom was like a dog who would have indigestion upon being happy or something as rude. We brothers were quiet and made Dad feel guilty and tried to comfort Mom with our superficial male words, the clerical tone of young men who have independent lives working on laptops.

Years later, my brother heard Dad speaking to someone on the phone, recommending feng shui this or that. He spoke in a confident tone detailing the maneuvers through the mysterious system and assured that it would bring upon his family: prosperity, well-being and happiness.

At which point my brother exploded: Not Happiness.

Amarkant Thakur
Khopoli, Maharashtra, India

ghazal

i sleep in the bedroom my dad built for someone else, the attic room where dreams come fast and feverish / if the moon is right, my sister and i can share dreams

of Camelot and sea caves, and the elephant tree; of homemade shortbread or of scissors and the dark place that exists only inside our mother / there, dreams

make as little sense to us as the language of our grandfather's lost homeland / we inherited everything from him but his tongue, his faith, his nightmare-dreams

of outer space and too-high tides and a border that bites; crosses his country; guts, devours, wounds, erases / instead we dream sweet dreams: short, fair-and-square dreams

where the sun never sets, never cowers, never burns our skin / in sleep we speak in secrets as soft and as sweet-smelling as spring / in the gold light, we pair dreams

like socks spread out across the landing; we balance them as we do East and West / when we sleep for the last time, the letter Z will die with us, we will wear dreams

that paint us gold / M, remember when they called you a prophet / wake up now in that bedroom, full of clothes you've outgrown, old birthday wishes, loose change, spare dreams

M. R. Massey
London

suite of gratitude
for Hugh Williams

:: I am holding in my hands the 1944 Modern Library
edition of *Twentieth-Century American Poetry,*
ed. Conrad Aiken.

The book is second-hand; a hardcover and has a dust-jacket
that's frayed at the upper-left-hand corner and the
upper part of the spine; the pages are yellowing.

The dust-jacket is protected/preserved by a creased
sheet of cellophane that wraps the outside of
this book's cover snugly. In pencil
is scrawled "1st," which stands for first-edition,
and right below is the price: "$4.75."
This is the exact copy of the book

I found on the shelf of the PhysEd room at Kingsbrook Jewish
Medical Center.
:: In the summer of 2007, I was struck by a train in Borough Park,
Brooklyn. To this day, I still don't have any idea as to how

I jumped in front of the train pulling into the station. After one month
of being unconscious in their ICU, I woke from a coma,
and my condition improved, slowly

and steadily. Thus I was moved to a regular ward of this
Brooklyn hospital. Everyday at around two
in the afternoon, a physical therapist

would come to my room and get me out of bed.
He'd help me practice how to walk again.
With a walker—the kind elderly

people use—I'd learn to put my legs back to working order.
Slowly, methodically, I was relearning how
to take one step at a time.

In this way, we'd make it to the PE room, the PT and I,
and this was where I came across the
20th-century poetry book.

:: My friend Hugh had made it a point to visit me every day of that first
month, even though I wasn't conscious. Everyday, he drove
from the Upper West Side of Manhattan

to Borough Park, Brooklyn. Hugh saw that I prized the borrowed
title, so a few days later he came in with the copy
I am now holding.

Hugh had ordered this Mod. Lib. edition online so that I
could have it and wouldn't have to borrow
the one from the PE room library.

:: Fast forward to three months later—when my wounds
healed and my over-all health improved,
Hugh offered to let me stay

at his one-room apartment near Columbia to recuperate. Seeing
that the area on my neck—between the collarbones
where the tracheotomy tube was inserted

—needed cleaning, Hugh listened to the doctor giving
directions and volunteered to wipe the wound,
apply a healing ointment,

and re-bandage the area. We had to do this every day. And everyday
while I was gaining back my strength in the apartment,
I looked forward to

the relief and feeling of cleanliness after Hugh wiped the wound.
:: How did our friendship begin? I met Hugh at
The Web, the gay bar where I danced as
a go-go boy. He was a regular at the bar. I remember
him coming in almost every day after work,
sitting at the bar,

ordering a drink and simply enjoying the beverage.
He then exchanged a $10 bill—sometimes
a $20—for dollar bills.

He came to the box where I was dancing and would
respectfully—
no other word for it—slip the bills inside my
underwear. When I worked nights,

when the club was packed with guys, Hugh came in and
sat at the bar whenever he could and without
fail, came by to say hi to me.

:: "[E]verything flickers / sexual and exquisite" is a fine phrase
from a multi-part poem by Muriel Rukeyser
I read from *Twentieth-Century*

American Poetry, seeing it as a precise and beautiful description
of the club scene (though MR is describing
something else altogether).

:: A month or two later, after I danced till 4 am, Hugh offered
to take me, in his car, to Chinatown for a hot meal.
I was often starving and broke
in Manhattan, Chinatown noodles were a respite from
50-cent per cup of noodles I got from the store.
:: Jamaica is known as the worst country

in the world for LGBTQ+ rights, but I ask you, how can Jamaica
produce a son as gentle as Hugh? :: I finished
Twentieth-Century American Poetry

in toto earlier this year—over a decade later—and I came across a short
poem by Ezra Pound, titled simply "Ité." I went East
to learn how to write.

The scars are with me till my dying days; the book—
a reminder. Listen to the fierce dignity and
high seriousness when Pound

says: "Go, my songs [...], / Seek ever to stand in the
hard Sophoclean light / And take your wounds
from it gladly."

Bingh
San Diego, California, USA

brooklyn summer curfew

The Brighton Beach rooftops purple
with June's slow dance sunset
thirty minutes past city curfew,
and from my rooftop, I phone film
the silent violence of my 8:30 PM
calm.

Below, a neighbor untethers
her hound uncorrected. She,
like me, doesn't know curfew
will lift tomorrow morning
like a strange fog.

name　　　　garden hermit　　　　pastoral　　　　name　　　　happy slave

　　myth　　　　　　plantation　　　　name　　Skid Row　　　tent

city problem　　　　name　　　　protest　　　　kidnaps　　　　patriotic

　　　name　　　　another Brooklyn　　　　　　policed

somewhere America　　shouts　　　names &　　　don't　　　shoot &

palms purple　　　with cop　　car　　flickering　　　red & blue

like　　in dependence　　　　day flash　bombs bursting　in　　tear

gas　　　　　　haze　　　&　　　　　　　　somewhere else

she is anonymous and likely
to cheek her usual pillow.

Someday, 2020's edges will fade,
like pocket stones or clouds
misnamed, into the taillights
of misdealt headlines, and other
stories we've told ourselves.

　　　　　　　　　　Danielle Zipkin
　　　　　　　　　　Brooklyn, New York

a space for mobility

Two bicycles, parallel
A woman, a man
Unhurried motion cuts through the wind

Hands holding, silent
A marriage of shadows
Timeless rotation consumes the single lane path

THIS IS NOT A PLACE FOR LOVE
I yell from behind
IT'S A SPACE FOR MOBILITY

>
> Angelo Zinna
> Amsterdam, Netherlands

realistic ways to break-up

I think we should eat our fried chicken
separately from now on.
You do not touch the spicy limbs
Without them being laden in hot sauce
And me?
my fingers burn when they and
green chilies are placed on the same kitchen table.
It's cheaper to eat alone, anyway.
And this, has been expensive.

Not that I had bet my money on this.
Maybe my heart, but never my money.
Because you can always recover a heart,
But the time and money spent here?
Do you know about the opportunity cost?
Maybe not, and that is what makes all the difference.
How do I spell out all the differences?
It's…not "Y-O-U" it's "M-E"

I think the "You" in my love poems is in desperate need of
A character makeover.
Or maybe a different role.
Or maybe just looking at the prospect of
Taking refuge, in poems
Which are not written by me.
I often get caught up on a random Sunday sunny afternoon
Wishing for a life different than what I didn't sign up for.
You, the one I signed up for.
But now I have forgotten the password to you.

Maybe we should go back to 'bros' or 'dude' or 'heyyyy' or 'hi I saw you today.'
Maybe put that day in my freezer
And think of ourselves
As people who have never touched each other, never noticed, never seen
Never known the feel of your suspicious mole right at the centre of your inner lip.
It can't be that difficult
Can it?
To strip yourself of a person's touch.
I will take showers every day.
Of course, alone.

I think our pets should find some other butts to sniff
I think we should look out for different future pets
Maybe as a precaution send pet memes as DMs to other people.
You never know who you end up jogging with.
And running is important you know?
Running into or away from you, how does it matter?

Let's admire the beauty from faraway
I never meant to get this close
So close, that you got under my skin
All the way to my nerves.
Let's label distance as space
Separation anxiety as excitement
Tears as happy tears
There are no happy tears, you will tell me.
But after the tears, you will be glad of leftover wet warmth
In the extra space of your bed, in the back seat of your bike,
In the specific places I would wait,
Definitely in our spot in front of my main gate.
I am scared of crossing even a road alone
So will you ask me to cross the bridge over this long distance?
You know I have never been good with directions and
How far will you search for my heart in the Google maps?

Maybe we should wait for each other
In places, we are bound to
Never run into each other.
Listen to unanswered calls at 2 a.m. when thunderstorm strikes
And leave aftermath messages saying
I wish I could see you right now.
Maybe in a distant universe
We should see each other
As parallel lines
That do not meet on this end of the paper. Or that end.
But somewhere in the infinity
Where time will be parallel to us and
We?
We will be infinite.

Shuvangi Khadka
Kathmandu, Nepal

broken eggs

It was eight in the morning, and my mother was making omelets.

She knew I hated omelets. But there she was anyways, humming quietly to herself as she took the brown carton from the fridge to place it next to the stove.

When I walked over to stand by her side, she rapped the egg against the edge of the sizzling pan, its sharp *crack* interrupting the 90s pop song sputtering from her old teal radio on the shelf. She brushed aside the blond curls spilling over one shoulder with a sunny smile as she poured the egg's guts onto the charcoal surface, lemon-yellow yolk grinning up at us as it deflated into the gooey white around it.

I could tell that breaking the eggs was her favorite part.

"You know, Marissa," she said knowingly to me, eyes flicking sideways as she flipped the spatula with a careful turn of her wrist, "In life, you gotta crack a few eggs to make a good omelet."

That was the stupidest expression I ever heard, and I made sure that she knew it. Of course you had to break eggs to make an omelet. That's how you made an omelet.

Her red-tipped hand, the one that wasn't holding the spatula, squished my cheeks together as she tipped her head back to laugh, flashing her perfect straight teeth. "You know what I mean, missy."

I did. But I didn't want to pretend she was wise, like she wanted me to. I wasn't in the mood.

I shoved her hand away and told her that I didn't want the good things in life to be omelets. In fact, I hated omelets, remember?

Bracelets, the long skinny oversize kind you get in a 5-pack at Target, clinked together on her left arm as she switched the heat off with a sudden movement, the blue-orange flames shrinking back under rusted cylinders. She scraped the finished omelet onto a polka-dotted plate that was sitting on the counter next to her and propped her hand on her waist to give me a wink, bopping my nose with the eggy spatula. "Good thing Mr. Richardson loves 'em!"

Mr. Richardson lived in the house across from us with his wife and four children. He drove a blue BMW and wore crazy colored ties for each day of the week and every morning before he went to work at his fancy law firm, I saw him kiss his wife goodbye on their front porch while I got ready for school.

Today was Saturday, so Mr. Richardson would be home alone while Mrs. Richardson took their kids to soccer practice. I had seen her pull out of their driveway in her faded forest green minivan about ten minutes ago.

From the way my mother carefully adjusted the fork on the plate and smoothed down the folds of her favorite red dress, I knew she had seen the minivan drive away too.

I followed behind her as she walked down the hallway to our front door and watched as she took a moment to rake back sunshine curls from her face in the mirror on the wall.

She glanced sideways at me and gave me one of her signature winning smiles, pulling me into a one-armed hug with the plate balanced on the fingertips of her other hand. The scent of her flowery perfume made my eyes water and forehead ache.

"Be good, missy. I'll be back soon!"

But she wasn't back soon.

It was nearly noon by the time I saw her close the Richardson's front door behind her, hands empty and dress hugging her figure as she strutted with square shoulders up our walkway.

The green minivan pulled into their driveway right after my mother locked our front door. It left soon after.

Two days later, on Monday morning, I watched from my bedroom window as Mr. Richardson, briefcase in hand and bright red polka dot tie loose around his neck, left his house for work without a kiss from his wife.

That night, my mother got a phone call with a job offer to work full-time as an assistant at a law firm. She had been searching for work for weeks after being let go at her previous job, so after dinner we celebrated with double chocolate cheesecake and vanilla ice cream.

"You know, Marissa," she said as she reclined against the wooden kitchen chair with a satisfied smile, sucking away the bits of chocolate that were stuck to her fork, "You can make a lot of things with broken eggs. Like cheesecake. It doesn't have to be all about omelets."

But I knew as I sat there across from my mother, dessert half-eaten and mind on the abandoned man across the street, that I didn't care what types of wonderful things broken eggs made. I'd never want to be the one to love to break them.

Cassidy Guimares
Boston, MA, USA

peachtree

After prom my friends and I went to the
Krispy Kreme on Peachtree Street,
a road built by Black convicts in
Old New South slavery, a backbone of
Atlanta named after the plantations.

We licked sheets of sugar off our lips,
wax-like and pinked by the lipstick we wore
to tell ourselves we knew about the world,
to tell the world we thought we knew about
that we could see it clearly under our false lashes.

I remember our eyelids heavy from their weight
or maybe we were just tired.

I don't remember the day after prom
but I'm sure I was sore from high heels, sure
I looked through the pictures of the
previous night, picking out the ones
that made me look older, taller,

the ones that made my eyebrows look smaller
and my hair look straighter, smoother.

Back then small eyebrows were *in* and
my friends told me to straighten my hair
but that didn't stop strangers from touching it.

Anyway, it would curl up as soon as I stepped
outside in Georgia air, unable to ignore its roots.

In prom pictures my friends and I stood in a line,
in a pattern of Black, white, Black, white so no one
could call us racists, *see look I have Black friends*
we could say if anyone asked but they never did.

After school those years my friends and I
would walk downtown and eat ice cream and
sit in the sun, leaning on an obelisk I would learn
years later was a Confederate monument.

I never knew because I never looked up.
I only looked down at the melting ice cream,
trying to catch it before it changed form.

My city tried to remove the obelisk but the state
said no and I think they tried to put a fence around it
but that didn't stop strangers from touching it,
spray painting it, hitting it, pushing it,
waging a new war for a *New* New South,
all of us strangers to our roots—or maybe
not as strange as we would like to think.

We, non-strangers would drive down Peachtree
every Sunday to a church where people soft and
empty like wax figures looked into nothing—
or maybe it was God—silently wishing to
do justice and walk humbly before clacking
their high heels into a reception hall for free
Krispy Kreme doughnuts before leaving

to beat the traffic and beat the rush and win,
I guess, to go home to their plantation-style houses
encircled by never-ending wraparound porches
sagging from the weight of their age, tired.

                              Miriam Moore-Keish
                              Atlanta, Georgia, USA

red pork soup

In thinking of my love of soup, I relax and close my eyes, a soup seance is about to begin. I summon a memory from several years ago. In Phuket, Thailand, trying to salvage a relationship with a man with whom I was no longer in love. Rather than call it quits, I decided a month alone together in a faraway place would be the solution. It took half a day to realise I was wrong and I found myself weeping down the phone to my mother begging to be saved. His love of Thailand, a country he had discovered as his marriage was failing, was odd to me. He spent most of the day in a local boxing gym, training for nothing; he was never going to be a fighter. I slept all night and all day, a helpful habit when I am depressed and don't wish to participate in the world; unconsciousness is a highly effective form of escapism. In the rare moments I was awake, I was tortured by a heat rash that had spread all over my body, an allergic reaction, I am certain, to the man I no longer loved. We fought, he boxed, I read, he stared at his phone, I cried, and we hardly had sex.

One night, he took me to a place by the side of a dusty road, where there was only one thing on the menu. As we pulled up on a motorcycle, I saw a diminutive woman standing behind a large vat with a man by her side. For romance's sake let's assume he was her husband - their vows intertwining them through sickness, health and soup. Their roles here were clearly defined. She: Mistress of the Stock. The most important part of any soup. Without it we are hopelessly drifting in water, floating in tastelessness hoping to be salvaged by salt. Clearly she understood this and thus dedicated herself to creating a broth so flavoursome you would have been quite satisfied had there been nothing else in your bowl. Certainly, her vast vessel was rarely cleaned; scarcely was the stock finished than it was simply added to over years, generations of women just like her refining the taste, trying to capture the essence of pig within its briny waters.

For his part, the husband was in charge of noodles, wantons and of course the pork that gave this soup its name. Beautiful in its simplicity and descriptiveness:

Red Pork Soup

We took our place at a vacant table, undisturbed by the ants that crawled all over the condiments. Two Red Pork Soups for a pair who were struggling to be together. I can't remember what we talked about over dinner, I do recall looking over at the man who loved me and realising in that moment that I must love him too. Although now I wonder if that was the soup talking, drunk as I was on the love of Red Pork Soup. I have the kind of distance from that relationship now, four years since it came to an end, that makes me sceptical of any real feeling. It is strange how you can love someone so much for a time and then find that those feelings not only recede and grow foggy, but often actually disappear altogether. I cannot recall the feeling of loving him - what it did to my body, whether he made my heart race, but I do remember the taste of Red Pork Soup. I know that when I bit into a wanton, a different, saltier broth filled my mouth, bursting out from deep within the parcel. I remember that as soon as we finished our bowls, slurping up the dregs by raising them up to our lips, we immediately ordered two more and devoured them with the same enthusiasm.

What am I trying to make sense of? That I love soup more than I love men, or at least that man? It's possible, I suppose. Soup has disappointed me, sure, but men have broken me. Soup has been too hot or too salty, men have been cold, violent, callous and unkind. Given the choice, I might stick with soup.

***

Something pulls me out of this dreamlike state. The smells and the tastes of Thailand begin to recede and I am catapulted back to the present. A familiar gnawing in my stomach brings me back from the Soup Seance and the memory I have summoned. I am hungry, I think, or perhaps the questions I had been asking myself were too uncomfortable to tackle. And so, fleeing, as I am wont to do, when I have committed myself to a day of writing. Deciding that it is lunchtime even though it is in fact 11:45am. Abandoning my laptop and my notebook, leaving them where they are on my desk because I believe The London Library is a sacred space and that my possessions will be quite safe, I walk out into the afternoon, stomping through Piccadilly, wondering where my legs are taking me. Our bodies know of our desires long before our brains are able to process the information and create the thought. It is only when I am already halfway there that I realise I am going to get soup. Of course. An attempt to nourish my soul, when the process of trying to put words on the page threatens to overwhelm me.

This place on Kingly St is practically a kiosk and it won't be there much longer. Another pop-up for a society unable to commit. The soup is fine, not really essay worthy, but it serves a purpose when only soup will do and you can't show your face at Prêt, for reasons I cannot now go into. Worryingly, there doesn't appear to be a kitchen attached in any way to the kiosk. The soup must have been transported that morning in insulated vats, delivered to the staff who stand there ladling the liquid into take away containers for hungry people who work nearby, chucking a few garnishes on top to give it a homemade feel. These people have no real connection to the soup they are serving, they haven't slaved over hot stoves, or been apprentice to an aging soup Sensei. The place purports to be sort of Jewish, but only because they sometimes serve Matzo Ball Soup. Today they are out, so I opt for a sweet potato situation which is pretty bland, but the bread is nice. Still, it's soup, and I am restored, if only for a moment.

The very next day, not satisfied by the previous offering, I find myself back at the soup place, prepared to give them one last chance. Today, they have what I want. Matzo Ball Soup. It is almost always a mistake to eat Matzo Ball Soup that hasn't been made by your Jewish mother. It is too engrained in your psyche, too associated with love and comfort and healing. My mother has only just mastered the careful balance required to make truly great kneidlach, but still, I'd take the slightly dry-in-the-middle dumplings of my childhood over whatever anyone else is offering. Also, the woman is a damn genius at making broth. But I'm a big girl now, I can't go running to mummy every time I want Chicken Soup. Well actually, I can, but she's on a yoga retreat in Valencia, so back to the soup kiosk I go. A friend, whose palate I respect, told me about this place, but crucially, she is not Jewish. That should have been the warning I needed to avoid the crushing disappointment I feel when faced with this sad excuse for MBS. The matzo balls themselves aren't all bad, although there is something about them that feels vaguely "wholegrain", as if they are trying to make them healthy. Listen, there is plenty of time in the day for virtuous eating, but a good matzo ball should be 96% schmaltz*, at least. If only that was the worst of it, but it is the broth in which they float that offends me most.

If I have not made my soup credentials clear, let me just say, I know good broth. The very word should conjure up images of big vats, painstakingly stirred by soup maestros, with chicken feet bobbing about, the surface, glistening with a thick layer of fat. Some witchcraft needs to be present, this cauldron of loveliness promises to heal you, to love you, it is an extension of your mother or grandmother, or any other caregiver, it is the nectar of their nurturing. I say all this to illustrate the seriousness of the issue. If you are selling me Matzo Ball Soup, you better make damned sure it tastes like chicken. These spelt balls are floating in boiled water with a little bit of coriander. This is akin to an anti-semitic hate crime.

I prefer to eat my chicken soup like this: precariously balanced on the arm of my parent's red sofa, worn through good use and the eager claws of a few generations of cats. I like to get rid of all the chicken first and then I can delight in the perfect roundness of the slices of carrot, grown soft from the cooking and reheating, the bits of leek that come apart and drift aimlessly around the bowl and the flecks of coriander that my mother refuses to serve it without. And then finally, to lift the bowl's rim to my lips and swallow the golden fluid down, just as I did with the Red Pork Soup, just as I do with all my soups. And almost always, while I methodically make my way through a bowl of chicken soup, I am being looked over by my mother, and I can feel the pleasure that she gets from seeing me eat a meal that she has prepared. A soup that her mother made for her and her mother before that. A recipe that survived the pogroms in the shtetls of

---

*My mother is very concerned that someone might take this gross exaggeration literally. A good matzo ball has far less schmaltz.

Lithuania and travelled to Cape Town, then to Zimbabwe and finally to London, where I sit slurping, being nourished in body and soul.

And that, perhaps, is the difference between all of these soups. Maybe the main issue with the soup kiosk on Kingly Street is that there are too many degrees of separation between soup and server. The crucial difference between the old Thai woman and the young person duty bound to ladle soup into cardboard bowls for busy Londoners on their lunch break, is that the woman in Phuket has poured her life into that soup, the kiosk worker is simply collecting a cheque. You can taste the difference, the soup lacks depth. And so too, might this explain the importance of my mother's chicken soup. I have never been to Lithuania, or South Africa, or the great many other countries my ancestors have been expelled from through centuries of persecution, but the taste of that particular soup roots me to the places I have never been, makes me feel, if only for a sip, that I belong.

***

With lunchtime soup slurped, I am back at the library to bring this tale to some sort of resolution. After the disastrous holiday, with only the momentary respite of Red Pork Soup, the love was over, the union doomed, this mini marriage I had played at for almost a year, where I was mainly asleep, needed to end. Appropriately, I used food as an excuse to start an argument and break things off. He asked me if I wanted a steak, I think, I said I didn't, a fight ensued and I said I couldn't do this anymore. Whatever that means. One of those tropes, when you can't find the courage to tell someone the truth. That you don't love them and you aren't sure you ever did. That you were so desperate to be held and touched, to be necessary to someone's happiness that you overlooked all the indications, present from the very start, that you were not at all compatible. That you had grown tired of contorting yourself into the person you thought they needed you to be, pretending to be interested in UFC and staying in and doing drugs together on a Friday night, having sex in the same position, and sleeping with the light on and the television blaring. That even though their love made you feel safe at times, you were beginning to detach from your body, you were starting to forget what you liked doing and eating and reading. Oftentimes the truth is cruel and it is easier simply to say, "I can't do this anymore", and hope that it is clear enough. Then perhaps to make the sort of promises we all make, that we will be friends and always be in each other's lives, though you hope they know you don't mean it. This is done. Maybe you won't be able to think about Thailand for a while, it is possible you will shudder every time someone mentions Conor McGregor and his upcoming fight, the smell of dope will cause you to come over a bit funny, that particular sensory memory evocative of the months you spent imprisoned in the Suburbs, but you know, as you leave this house of his that you never felt you belonged in, that if you ask her to, your mother will make you some Chicken Soup. And after you've finished it, when only the flecks of coriander remain in the bowl, she'll run her thumb across your forehead in that way she does. As you cry with a sense of shame, because you caused this pain, you hurt someone kind and loving and you don't feel entitled to your tears. The taste of chicken and matzo balls still caressing your mouth, it isn't new and exciting like Red Pork Soup, you've had this dish countless times, but it is medicinal, and you permit yourself to believe, even if only for the briefest moment, that you might have made the right decision and you will be ok.

I am certain that it takes a lifetime to learn how to make soup properly, my own are thin and often flavourless. Though my mother scolds me each time she boils a chicken and tells me that I must pay attention, that one day I may well become the Jewish matriarch comforting needy children and tending to broken hearts, I still don't know how to do it. She loses me somewhere between removing the carcass and straining the fluid, I suppose I think I'll learn how to do it by eating it, or by thinking about it. I like the idea though, that I can be someone you call upon when you are sick and need to be taken care of, that I can be someone's mum. When my mother comforts me and holds me to her, I inhale deeply and to me, she always smells of chicken soup. Right now I am just collecting material, sourcing all the experiences I need to one day pour into my own soup so that I might be that chicken-scented person to someone, or so that I might be better able to selfsoothe. I'm picturing myself fifty years in the future, old lady, vast bosom, several wiry chin hairs, but still somehow unshakeably glamorous, comforting a younger version of myself, but I'm not there yet. Maybe it's like singing the blues, you have to have had your heart broken a thousand times before you are able to do it justice.

Francesca Leonie
London, England

> "If the stars shine at night
> then surely someone needs them?"
> from *Listen!*, by V.V. Mayakovsky

but listen to this –
for if we look out to the stars at night
                          then surely they too need us?
Surely
those sparkles of dust need to know
they do not shine for themselves alone?
That they,
       like a child
grip to the bars of the cot
and their light –
          the cry
for the mother to finally utter -
"no! you are not forgotten"?
Or us resided smokers
firefly over a bench
think of it as no more –
than bad habit.
But to them –
               we're a whole constellation.
And what if their dying light
needs to enter our eye
and rustle into our mind
before igniting the fickle flame of memory
and finally be mapped with graphite
and told how they belong
to themselves,
to us,
to all that's known.
And just before we depart,
as the dark resides over our gaze
these stars appear to say
"thank you – for letting us know
we do not shine for ourselves alone."

                      Alex Fadeev
              London, United Kingdom

Printed in Great Britain
by Amazon